SUNDAY
SUNDAES

SUNDAY SUNDAES

Coco Simon

Simon Spotlight

New York   London   Toronto   Sydney   New Delhi

SIMON SPOTLIGHT

An imprint of Simon & Schuster Children's Publishing Division

1230 Avenue of the Americas, New York, New York 10020

This Simon Spotlight edition May 2018

Copyright © 2018 by Simon & Schuster, Inc.

All rights reserved, including the right of reproduction in whole or in part in any form.

SIMON SPOTLIGHT and colophon are registered trademarks of Simon & Schuster, Inc.

Text by Liz Carey

For information about special discounts for bulk purchases, please contact Simon & Schuster Special Sales at 1-866-506-1949 or business@simonandschuster.com.

Designed by Hannah Frece

The text of this book was set in Bembo Std.

Manufactured in the United States of America 0318 OFF

10 9 8 7 6 5 4 3 2 1

ISBN 978-1-5344-1747-2 (hc)

ISBN 978-1-5344-1746-5 (pbk)

ISBN 978-1-5344-1748-9 (eBook)

Library of Congress Catalog Card Number 2018934107

CHAPTER ONE
PLOT TWIST

A hot August wind lifted my brown hair and cooled the back of my neck as I waited for the bus to take me to my new school. I hoped I was standing in the right spot. I hoped I was wearing the right thing. I wished I were anywhere else.

My toes curled in my new shoes as I reached into my messenger bag and ran my thumb along the worn spine of my favorite book. I'd packed *Anne of Green Gables* as a good-luck charm for my first day at my new school. The heroine, Anne Shirley, had always cracked me up and given me courage. To me, having a book around was like having an old friend for company. And, boy, did I need a friend right about now.

Ten days before, I'd returned from summer camp

to find my home life completely rearranged. It hadn't been obvious at first, which was almost worse. The changes had come out in drips, and then all at once, leaving me standing in a puddle in the end.

My mom and dad picked me up after seven glorious weeks of camp up north, where the temperature is cool and the air is sweet and fresh. I was excited to get home, but as soon as I arrived, I missed camp. Camp was fun, and freedom, and not really worrying about anything. There was no homework, no parents, and no little brothers changing the ringtone on your phone so that it plays only fart noises. At camp this year I swam the mile for the first time, and all my camp besties were there. My parents wrote often: cheerful e-mails, mostly about my eight-year-old brother, Tanner, and the funny things he was doing. When they visited on Parents' Weekend, I was never really alone with them, so the conversation was light and breezy, just like the weather.

The ride home was normal at first, but I noticed my parents exchanging glances a couple of times, almost like they were nervous. They looked different too. My dad seemed more muscular and was tan, and my mom had let her hair—dark brown and wavy, like mine—grow longer, and it made her look younger. The minute I got home, I grabbed my sweet cat, Diana (named after Anne Shirley's best friend, naturally), and scrambled into my room. Sharing a bunkhouse with eleven other girls for a summer was great, but I was really glad to be back in my own quiet room. I texted SHE'S BAAAACK! to my best friends, Tamiko Sato and Sierra Perez, and then took a really long, hot shower.

It wasn't until dinnertime that things officially got weird.

"You must've really missed me," I said as I sat down at the kitchen table. They'd made all of my favorites: meat lasagna, garlic bread, and green salad with Italian dressing and cracked pepper. It was the meal we always had the night before I left for camp and the night I got back. My mouth started watering.

I grinned as I put my napkin onto my lap.

"We *did* miss you, Allie!" said my mom brightly.

"They talked about you all the time," said Tanner, rolling his eyes and talking with his mouth full of garlic bread, his dinner napkin still sitting prominently on the table.

"Napkin on lapkin!" I scolded him.

"Boys don't use napkins. That's what sleeves are

3

for," said Tanner, smearing his buttery chin across the shoulder of his T-shirt.

"Gross!" Coming out of the all-girl bubble of camp, I had forgotten the rougher parts of the boy world. I looked to my parents to reprimand him, but they both seemed lost in thought. "Mom? Dad? Hello? Are you okay with this?" I asked, looking to both of them for backup.

"Hmm? Oh, Tanner, don't be disgusting. Use a napkin," said my mom, but without much feeling behind it.

He smirked at me, and when she looked away, he quickly wiped his chin on his sleeve again. It was like all the rules had flown out the window since I'd been gone!

My dad cleared his throat in the way he usually did when he was nervous, like when he had to practice for a big sales presentation. I looked up at him; he was looking at my mom with his eyebrows raised. His bright blue eyes—identical to mine—were *definitely* nervous.

"What's up?" I asked, the hair on my neck prickling a little. When there's tension around, or sadness, I can always feel it. It's not like I'm psychic or anything.

I can just feel people's feelings coming off them in waves. Maybe my parents' fighting as I was growing up had made me sensitive to stuff, or maybe it was from reading so many books and feeling the characters' feelings along with them. Whatever it was, my mom said I had a lot of empathy. And right now my empathy meter was registering *high alert*.

My mom swallowed hard and put on a sunny smile that was a little too bright. Now I was really suspicious. I glanced at Tanner, but he was busy dragging a slab of garlic bread through the sauce from his second helping of lasagna.

"Allie, there's something Dad and I would like to tell you. We've made some new plans, and we're pretty excited about them."

I looked back and forth between the two of them. What she was saying didn't match up with the anxious expressions on their faces.

"They're getting divorced," said Tanner through a mouthful of lasagna and bread.

"What?" I said, shocked, but also . . . kind of not. I felt a huge sinking in my stomach, and tears pricked my eyes. I knew there had been more fighting than usual before I'd left for camp, but I hadn't really seen

5

this coming. Or maybe I had; it was like divorce had been there for a while, just slightly to the side of everything, riding shotgun all along. Automatically my brain raced through the list of book characters whose parents were divorced: Mia in the Cupcake Diaries, Leigh Botts in *Dear Mr. Henshaw*, Karen Newman in *It's Not the End of the World*. . . .

My mother sighed in exasperation at Tanner.

"Wait, Tanner knew this whole time and I didn't?" I asked.

"Sweetheart," said my dad, looking at me kindly. "This has been happening this summer, and since Tanner was home with us, he found out about it first." Tanner smirked at me, but Dad gave him a look. "I know this is hard, but it's actually really happy news for me and your mom. We love each other very much and will stay close as a family."

"We're just tired of all the arguing. And we're sure you two are too. We feel that if we live apart, we'll be happier. All of us."

My mind raced with questions, but all that came out was, "What about me and Tanner? And Diana? Where are we going to live?"

"Well, I found a great apartment right next to the

6

playground," said my dad, suddenly looking happy for real. "You know that new converted factory building over in Maple Grove, with the rooftop pool that we always talk about when we pass by?"

"And I've found a really great little vintage house in Bayville. And you won't believe it, but it's right near the beach!"

I stared at them.

Mom swallowed hard and kept talking. "It's just been totally redone, and the room that will be yours has built-in bookcases all around it and a window seat," she said.

"And it has a hot tub," added my dad.

"Right," laughed my mom. "And there are plant-ings in the flower beds around the house, so we can have fresh flowers all spring, summer, and fall!" My mom loved flowers, but my dad grew up doing so much yard work for his parents that he refused to ever let her plant anything here. The house did sound nice, but then something occurred to me.

"Wait, Bayville and Maple Grove? So what about school?" Bayville was ten minutes away!

"Well." My parents shared a pleased look as my mom spoke. "Since my new house is in Bayville, you qualify for seventh grade at the Vista Green School! It's the top-rated school in the district, and it's gorgeous! Everything was newly built just last year. Tan will go to MacBride Elementary."

"Isn't that great?" said my dad.

"Um, *what*? We're changing *schools*?" The lasagna was growing cold on my plate, but how could I eat? I looked at Tanner to see how he was reacting to all this news, but he was nearly finished with his second helping of lasagna and showed no sign of stopping. The shoulder of his T-shirt now had red sauce stains smeared across it. I looked back at my mom.

"Yes, sweetheart. I know it will be a big transition at first. Everything is going to be new for us all! A fresh start!" said my mom enthusiastically.

Divorce. Moving. A new school.

"Is there any *more* news?" I asked, picking at a crispy corner of my garlic bread.

"Actually," my mom began, looking to my dad, "I have some really great news. Dad and I decided it probably wasn't a good idea for me to go on being the chief financial officer of his company. So I've rented a space in our new neighborhood, and . . . I'm opening an ice cream store, just like I've always dreamed!

Ta-da!" She threw her arms wide and grinned.

My jaw dropped as I lifted my head in surprise. "Really?" My mom made the best—I mean the absolute *best*—homemade ice cream in the world. She made a really thick, creamy ice cream base, and then she was willing to throw in anything for flavor: lemon and blueberries, crumbled coffee cake, crushed candy canes, you name it. She was known for her ice cream. I mean, people came to our house and actually asked if she had any in the freezer.

My mom was nodding vigorously, the smile huge on her face. She looked happier and younger than I'd seen her in years. And my dad looked happier than he had in a long time.

"And you two can be the taste testers!" said my mom.

"Yessss!" said Tanner, pumping his fist out and back against his chest. "And our friends, too?" he asked.

"Yes. All of your friends can test flavors too," said my mom.

"Okay, wait." I couldn't take this all in at once. It felt like someone had removed my life and replaced it with a completely new version.

Who were these people? What was my family? *Who was I?*

"Eat your dinner, honey," urged my dad. "It's your favorite. There's plenty of time to talk through all of this."

My eyes suddenly brimmed with tears; I just couldn't help it. Even if—and this was a big "if" for me—this would be a good move for our family, there was still a new house and a new *school*. What about my friends? What about Book Fest, the reading cele-bration at my school that I helped organize and was set to run this year?

I wiped my eyes with my sleeve. "What about Book Fest?" I said meekly.

My mom stood and came around to hug me. "Oh, Allie, I'm sure they'll still let you come."

I pulled away. "Come? I *run* it! Who's going to run it now? And what will I do instead?"

I scraped my chair away from the table, pulled away from my mom, and raced to my room. Diana was curled up on my bed, and she jumped when I closed the door hard behind me. (It wasn't a slam, but almost.) I grabbed Diana, flopped onto the bed, and had a good cry. Certainly Anne Shirley would have thrown herself onto her bed and cried, at least at first. But what would Hermione Granger have done? Violet Baudelaire? Katniss Everdeen? My favorite characters encountered a lot of troubles, but they usually got through them okay, and it wasn't by lying around crying about them. I sniffed and reached for a tissue, and slid up against my headboard into a sitting position so that I could have a good think, like a plot analysis.

My parents had been unhappy for a long time. I kind of knew that. I mean, I guess we were all unhappy because Mom and Dad fought a lot.

They both worked hard at their jobs, and I knew they were tired, so I always thought a lot of it was just crankiness. Plus Mom was the business manager and my dad ran the marketing group at their company, so I figured since they worked together all day, they just got on each other's nerves after work. But if I really thought about it, I realized that they were like that on the weekends, and even on holidays and vacations. They snapped at each other. They rolled their eyes. And sometimes one of them stomped out of the room. And the more I thought about it, I realized they hadn't spent a lot of time together over the past year. Either Mom would be taking me to soccer and Dad would be staying home with Tanner, or Dad would be doing carpool and errands while Mom went with Tanner to his music lessons. We always ate dinner together, but starting last winter and right up to when I'd left for camp, there had been a lot of pretty quiet meals, with each of us lost in our own thoughts. Mom would talk to me or to Tanner, and Dad would always ask about our days, but they never actually spoke to each other.

I squeezed my eyes shut and tried to think of the last time we'd all been happy together. The night before I left for camp, maybe? We had my favorite dinner, and Dad was teasing that it would be the last great meal before I ate camp food for the summer. Mom joked that we should sneak some lasagna into my shoes, which Tanner thought was a really good idea. Dad ran and picked up one of my sneakers, and Mom pretended to spoon some in. We were being silly and laughing, and I felt warm and snug and cozy. I loved camp and couldn't wait to go every year, but I remembered thinking right then that I'd miss being at the table with my family around me.

Later that night, though, I heard Mom and Dad

fighting about something in their room, like they seemed to do almost every night. Then for seven weeks I went to sleep hearing crickets and giggles instead of angry whispers, along with a few warnings of "Girls, it's time to go to bed!" from my counselors.

Now I heard whispers from Mom and Dad on the other side of the door. They weren't angry, but they didn't sound happy, either. Then I heard the whispers fade as they went downstairs.

I guess I fell asleep, because when I woke up, Dad was sitting on my bed and Mom was standing next to him, looking worried. The lights were out, but my room was bright from the moon.

"Allie," Dad said gently. "You need to brush your teeth and get ready for bed."

"Do you want to talk about anything?" Mom asked as I sat up.

Suddenly I was really annoyed. "Oh, you mean like how you decided to get a divorce and not tell me? Or sell our house and not tell me? Or that I would need to move schools and totally start over again? Nope, nothing to discuss at all." I crossed my arms over my chest.

"Allie," Mom said, and her voice broke. I could

tell she was upset, but I didn't care. "We are divorcing because we think it will make us happier. All of us."

"Speak for yourself," I said. I knew I was being mean, and on any usual day one of them would tell me to watch my tone.

"It is going to be hard," said Dad slowly. "It's going to be an adjustment, and it's going to take a lot of patience from all of us. We are not sugar-coating that part. But it's going to be better. You and Tanner mean everything to us, and Mom and I are going to do what will make you happiest. This separation will make us stronger as a family. Things will be better, and we need you to believe that."

"And what if I don't?" I said. I knew I was on thin ice. Even I could tell that I sounded a little bratty. "What will make me happiest is to stay in this house and go to the same school with my friends and . . ." I thought about it for a second. "Wait, if I'm moving to Bayville, when will I ever see Dad?"

"A lot still needs to be worked out," said Mom. "For now you and Tanner and Diana will live with me at the house in Bayville during the week. Dad will come over every Wednesday, and every other weekend you'll be at Dad's apartment in Maple Grove."

I looked at Dad. "So every other week I'll only see you on Wednesdays?" I felt my eyes filling with tears again.

"We can work things out, Allie," said Dad quickly. "I am still here and I am still your dad and I will always be around."

"I promise you, Allie, we're going to do everything we can to make this better for all of us," Mom said. I couldn't see her face clearly, but I could see that she was trying hard not to cry.

Dad reached over and gave Mom's arm a little squeeze. I sat there looking at them, not being able to remember the last time I'd seen Mom give Dad a kiss hello, or Dad hug Mom. Now here they were, but even that didn't seem right.

"I'm not brushing my teeth," I said. I don't really know why I said that. I guess I just wanted to feel like I was still in control of something, anything. Then I turned away from them and pulled up the covers. All I wanted to do was go to sleep, because I was really hoping I would wake up and this would all be a bad dream.

I woke up and blinked a few times, remembering that I was back in my room at home and not still at camp. Well, home for now.

I slowly got up and listened at the door. I could hear Mom talking and the *clink* of a spoon in a bowl, which meant Tanner was slurping his cereal. I didn't want to stay in my room, but I didn't want to go downstairs either. I grabbed my phone. With all of the drama the night before, I had completely forgotten to check it. I looked at the screen, and there were eighteen messages, ranging from did a big scary monster eat you???? to OMG she came back and now she's gone again! from my best friends, Tamiko and Sierra. I sent a couple of quick texts to them, and within seconds my phone was buzzing, as I'd known it would be.

Just then Mom knocked at my door and opened it. "Good morning, sweetie!" she said with her new Sally Sunshine voice that I was already not liking. "I'm so glad to have my girl home!"

I looked at her. Was she just going to pretend nothing had happened?

Mom came in and sat down on my bed. "Dad

left for work, but I took this week off. The movers are coming in a couple of days, and we'll need time to settle into our new house." She looked at me. I stared at the wall. The wall of my room, where I had lived since I was a baby. I looked at the spot behind the door, and Mom followed my eyes. She sighed. Since I had been tiny, Dad had measured me on the wall on my birthday and had made a little mark at the top of my head. He'd even done it last year, even though I'd told him I was way too old. "I'm going to miss this house," she said softly. "It has a lot of memories."

It was quiet for a second. Mom looked like she was far away.

"You took your first steps in the kitchen," she said, really smiling this time. "And remember your seventh birthday party that we had in the backyard?" I did. It was a fairy tea party, and each kid got fairy wings and a magic wand. There had been so many birthdays and holidays in this house.

I had never lived in another house. All I knew was this one. I knew that there were thirty-eight steps between the front porch and the bus stop. I could run up the stairs to the second floor in eight seconds

(Tanner and I had timed each other), and I knew that the cabinet door in the kitchen where we kept the cookies creaked when you opened it.

"I think you'll like the new house," said Mom. "Houses. You'll have two homes."

I looked straight ahead.

"Your new room has bookcases all around it. I thought of you when I saw it and knew you would love it." Mom looked at me. "And there's a really great backyard to hang out in. I'm thinking about getting a hammock maybe, and definitely some comfy rocking chairs."

"What about my new other house?" I asked.

"Well," Mom said, "Dad's house is an apartment, actually, and it has really cool views. It's modern, and my house is more old-fashioned. It's the best of both worlds!"

I sighed.

Mom sighed. "Honey, I know this is tough."

I still didn't answer. Mom stood up.

"Well, kiddo, we have a lot to do. I'm guessing Tamiko and Sierra are coming over soon?"

I looked at my phone lighting up. "Maybe," I said.

Mom nodded. "Okay. Well, let me know what

you want to do today. It's your first day back. Tomorrow, though, we do need to pack up your room. Dad and I have been packing things up for the past few weeks, but there's still a lot to do."

I looked into the hall. I must have missed the fact that there were some boxes stacked there. One was marked "Mom" and one was marked "Dad."

Mom followed my gaze. "We're trying to make sure there are familiar things in each house. You can split up your room or . . . I was thinking maybe you'd like to get a new bedroom set?" There was that fake bright happy voice again.

I looked around the room. I liked my room. If the house couldn't stay the same, at least my room could. "No," I said. "I want this stuff."

"We should also talk about your new school," Mom said.

I looked down at my feet. My toenails were painted in my camp colors, blue and yellow. I wiggled them.

"You're already enrolled, but I talked to the principal about having you come over to take a tour and maybe meet some of your new teachers."

I shrugged.

"I think it might be good to take a ride over, just

so you are familiar with it before your first day," she said. "It's a bigger school, so you could get the lay of the land. And I've been asking around the new neighborhood, and there are a few girls who will be in your grade."

I nodded.

"Okay," she said brightly. "Well, we have this week to do that, so we'll just find a good time to go."

I swallowed hard.

Mom stood in the doorway and waited a minute, then stepped back into the room quickly, gathered me up in her arms, and hugged me tightly. "It's going to be better, baby girl," she said, kissing the top of my head like she used to when I was little. She was using her normal voice again. "I promise you, it might be hard, but it's definitely going to be better."

I tried really, really hard not to cry. A few tears spilled out, and Mom wiped them away. She took my face in her hands and looked at me. "Now," she said, "first things first, because I think there's a griddle that's calling our names."

I knew the tradition, so I had to smile.

"Welcome-back pancakes!" we said at the same time. Mom's blueberry pancakes were my welcome-

20

home-from-camp tradition. She always put ice cream on them to make them into smiley faces and wrote "XO" in syrup on my plate. I could already taste them. I stood up and followed Mom downstairs. Maybe she was right about things. This day was already getting a little bit better.

The next couple of days were a blur. On our last night in the house, we sat on the grass in the backyard. We had been packing and hauling boxes, and we were all sweaty and dirty and tired. Mom and Dad had emptied out the refrigerator and cabinets, so we had kind of a mishmash to eat. Tanner was eating cereal, peanut butter, crackers, and a hot dog that Dad had made on the grill. For dessert Mom pulled out the last carton of ice cream from the freezer, and since we had packed the bowls up, we all stuck spoons in and shared. "Hey!" I yelped as Tanner's spoon jabbed mine.

"I want those chocolate chips!" he said, digging in. Mom laughed. "In about a week we're going to have so much ice cream, we won't even know what to do with it!" Mom's store was opening soon, and since she was so busy with all the details, the packing at home hadn't exactly gone smoothly. Since Mom kept having to go to the store for things like the freezer delivery or to meet with people about things like what kind of spoons to order, we actually got Dad's apartment set up first. It was nice, but it was . . . well, weird. Tanner and I each had our own rooms, but they were kind of small. And Dad's house felt like Dad's, not really like our house. Dad had always loved modern things, so everything was glass and leather. It looked like it should be in a catalog. I was kind of afraid to mess anything up. There were a lot of pictures of me and of Tanner, but the first thing I noticed was that there were no pictures of the four of us.

"Where's the one from New Year's?" I asked, standing in front of a bookcase. We always took a family picture on New Year's Day.

Dad looked around. "Oh," he said, a little flustered. "I guess Mom took those shots. She has more room in the house."

I looked at him. *So this is how it's going to be,* I thought. *The three of us here and the three of us there.*

"We can take some new shots!" Dad said.

"Better," I kept whispering to myself. They'd both promised it was going to be better. But it wasn't really better. It was just downright weird.

The night before moving day, Tanner and I went to bed late. We had been packing all day, and we were beat, but I still couldn't sleep. I heard the back door open. I looked out my window and saw a shadow on the lawn. I almost freaked out, but then I realized that it was Mom, sitting on one of the rocking chairs that we'd bought for the new house but that had accidentally gotten delivered here. She was facing the house, and she looked like she was trying to memorize exactly the way it looked right then. I wondered if she could see me looking out at her. Then I saw Dad walk toward her. It was kind of weird that he was still here, since he had his apartment already, but they had decided that we would all move at the same time. Dad sat down on the grass next to Mom, and I could see them talking but couldn't hear what they were saying. I heard Mom laugh, and then I heard Dad laughing too. It was a nice sound. It was the last night we'd all be sleeping in this house together. I knew we were still a family—they kept telling us that—but it was the last time we'd all live together, and tomorrow morning everything was going to really change. I looked at

Mom and Dad laughing, but all it did was make my throat thick. Some things were too sad to see, so I flung myself into bed, hoping I'd fall asleep fast.

When the movers rolled up to the house early the next morning, Mom and Dad had already been up for hours, cleaning and sweeping and taking care of a lot of last-minute stuff. The house already didn't look like ours anymore.

When everything was loaded up, Mom locked the front door and handed Dad the key. We all stood there on the porch for a minute, looking up at the house. *Home.* I started to cry, and so did Mom. I buried my head in Dad's chest, and I could tell he was crying too. Only Tanner, who was sitting on the step playing a game on Dad's phone, seemed unmoved. "Tanner!" I yelled. "Say good-bye to your house!"

Tanner looked up, confused. "Uh, bye, house," he said, and we all laughed.

"Okay, troops," Mom said. "Onward." Tanner and I got into Mom's car, and we pulled out of the driveway. I looked back down our street as long as I could, saying good-bye to everything as it was.

We turned onto the main road, and Mom took a

deep breath. "Okay, gang," she said. "On to our next adventure! Here we go."

"To where?" Tanner asked.

"To our new house," Mom said, turning around to look at Tanner. "And to better things ahead."

"Oh," said Tanner. "I thought maybe we were going someplace fun." Mom looked at Tanner like he had ten heads. Then she looked at me, and we both cracked up. Some things, it seemed, weren't going to change at all.

CHAPTER TWO

THE PLOT THICKENS

I hadn't taken a bus to school in years. And even then, I'd had Tamiko and Sierra, and sometimes Sierra's twin sister, Isabel, to sit with. But here I was on the first day of my new school, stepping onto a big yellow bus. Mom had asked if I wanted to be driven to school, but I thought that might be more embarrassing. Mom had taken me to the new school the week before, and I met the principal and we walked around a little bit. I'd really wanted to meet the librarian, but she wasn't there that day. The school seemed fine but big. I was a little nervous about finding my way around, but the principal had given me a map, and Mom and Dad and I had looked at it together the night before.

Mom had started a kind of annoying ritual of after-dinner walks in the new neighborhood. I didn't mind the walking part, but Mom kept stopping to introduce herself to people and talk to them, which was really embarrassing. If she saw that they had a kid who looked remotely like they were my age or Tanner's, she practically marched up their front lawn. One night she spotted three girls my age getting out of a car. She called out "Hello!" before I could beg her not to.

"Hi! I'm Meg!" she said, smiling at the woman who got out of the driver's seat. "We just moved in on Bayberry Lane!"

"Oh, hi!" said the woman. "I'm Jill. This is my daughter Blair and her friends Maria and Palmer."

Blair gave me the once-over. Mom and I had been arranging furniture all day, so I was just wearing an old tank top and shorts. Blair and her friends were wearing cute outfits. Blair nodded at me, then said loudly, "We'll be inside. Bye!" She wiggled her fingers, and then her friends followed her to the house.

I hadn't exactly been expecting an invitation or anything, but Blair's mom said, "Oh my goodness. Well, Allie just moved here and would probably love to hang out too. Allie, would you like to come in? The girls are going to watch a movie."

"Oh, no," I said quickly.

Mom looked confused. "I can come pick you up later," she said.

"Or I can just run you home," Jill said.

"Maybe another time," I said, smiling. "Thank you."

"You are always welcome to drop by," said Jill. She looked behind her and seemed surprised to see that Blair had already gone inside.

Mom chattered on for a few more minutes while I looked down at my feet. "Mooom," whined Tanner. "I want to go hooome."

Jill laughed. "So sorry to keep you. We'll see you again soon!"

She and Mom exchanged phone numbers, and then Mom bounced down the driveway. "Isn't that great?" Mom said. "We just met three girls who will be with you at your new school!"

Yeah, I thought. *Absolutely wonderful.*

Now as I walked down the bus aisle, looking at all the unfamiliar faces staring up at me, I could feel my heart thudding and my face reddening. There weren't any empty seats in the front, and anyway, all the kids there looked younger than me. Toward the back, Blair, Maria, and Palmer were in two rows, one behind the other, all chatting with their heads bent together. They reminded me of me, Tamiko, and Sierra, and seeing them felt like a stab to the heart, but I headed toward them, seeking familiar territory.

They were pretty but not overly done up. Maybe they'd be my new friends? Maybe we'd all just gotten off on the wrong foot? As I drew closer, the bus lurched into motion and I was thrown toward the empty spot beside Blair. In a split-second decision, I started to sit down there, but all three girls looked up at me with such cold, withering stares that I gulped and turned to the closest seat. It was next to a boy who sat looking steadfastly out the window. He didn't even look at me as I sat down, but the girls turned to see where I'd landed and then put their heads back together, whispering and laughing. I'd never experienced "mean girls" in real life, only in books and movies, and I couldn't believe this was really happening to me.

My face flamed again, and I was momentarily filled with a surge of pure, white-hot anger at my parents. This new-school thing was not going to be easy, and it was all their fault!

Right then my phone buzzed, and I pulled it out to see that I had a new SuperSnap from Tamiko. Relief spread through my veins; I *did* have friends. In my old school I'd been popular, so take *that*, mean girls!

I opened the snap and studied the photo of Tamiko and Sierra in Mr. Sato's car on their way to school. It said Miss ya, Sistah! and had a big lipstick-kiss emoji on it. I knew they meant well, but it actually made me feel worse. Quickly I silenced the notifications, locked my phone, and slid it back into my bag. My fingers grazed *Anne of Green Gables* again. I wished I could pull out the comforting and familiar book, but to read something on the bus on the first day would probably just be asking for a snicker. I closed my eyes and took a deep breath, then let it out slowly like I'd learned in our mindfulness unit last year. I did it two more times, and then I let my eyes flutter open.

Yup. Still on the bus.

It was going to be a long day.

Okay, my mom was right about one thing: my new school was *super*-beautiful. I had gotten a small taste of it when I took the school tour, but now I couldn't help admiring all the swooping open spaces and comfy lounge areas—skylights, and terraces with seating, and plants everywhere. The lockers were all newish and smelled good, and the halls were carpeted so that it wasn't a total racket when kids were milling around on their way to class. I had to admit that Vista Green was waaaaay nicer than my old school.

The only problem was that it was really hard to find your way around. I mean, there were no straight hallways. Nothing lined up, nothing made sense, and from minute one, I was lost. I stood in the hall, my bag slung over my shoulder, slowly turning in a circle as I tried to orient myself using the map that the principal had given me. The locker combo they'd given me had worked fine, the schedule they'd given me was very clear, and the office ladies had been pretty nice. But I could not figure out where I needed to go. I tried walking one way, and the room numbers went in the opposite direction of what I'd expected. So I tried walking the other way, but those rooms had letters and not numbers on them. And with each step I took, fewer and fewer kids were walking on the soft sage-green carpeting. I was going to be late.

Just as I was about to give up and walk back to the office, I spied Blair. My stomach clenched as I looked around for someone—*anyone*—else to ask for directions from. I clutched the now-damp corners of the map and stared intently at it, hoping she would just pass me by, but she didn't.

"Hey, new girl, are you lost?" she asked.

I looked up. She was looking at me curiously but not meanly. Maybe this was one of those things where the girls were nice when they were apart but not so nice when they were together; I'd read books where that was what happened. There was no way to avoid speaking to her, and anyway she was my last hope, so I took a deep breath and said, "Do you know how to get to the science lab, room C243, by any chance?"

She hesitated for a split second, and I braced myself for a mean comment. But instead she grinned widely and said, "Sure! It's easy. Head down to the lower level—that's two flights down—and it's right past the pool on your right! You can't miss it." She flounced off.

"Okay, thanks!" I called after her, and I set off down the stairs in relief.

I was wandering the lowest level, peeking in

through the doorway of what turned out to be an empty English classroom, when a series of quiet chimes rang out. I guessed that was Vista Green's version of the earsplitting jangle that signaled the start and end of classes at my old school—also an improvement.

I was just pulling open the door of what might have been a laboratory, or a library—through the window I could see rows of desks with computers—when I heard a stern voice.

"Are you meant to be in class, young lady?"

I turned quickly and found myself face-to-face with a tiny, middle-aged woman, her dark hair long and wavy, a pair of funky rectangular glasses perched on her nose. She was dressed in a chic batik dress with a wide braided leather belt.

"I—I—" I stammered, holding the map out toward her. "I'm lost."

Her expression softened, just slightly. "Oh, you're new. Where are you meant to be? Let's see." In relief I held out the schedule to her.

"Tsk, tsk!" she tutted. "You're way off. The science labs are all the way on the third floor. How on earth did you end up down here?" She sighed heavily. "I'd better take you up in the elevator." She began walking briskly up the hall, her slingback heels scuffing the carpet, as she talked a mile a minute. "I'm Mrs. K. I'm the librarian; that was the library; lowest level is library and English. Reading is very important here at Vista Green; all students must have an independent reading book at all times so that you can Drop Everything and Read. You know, *D-E-A-R*? If you don't have a book, come see me. . . ."

We hopped into the elevator, and she continued her chatter. I tried to answer what seemed like questions (yes, I had an independent reading book; no, I didn't have English class until tomorrow), but it was as if she didn't really need the answers. She was on a roll.

The elevator pinged on the third floor and the doors opened.

"Take a left, then a right; it's on your right. Off you go now. No dillydallying!"

"Thank you. I'm Allie Shear," I said as I backed away down the hall.

"I know!" she said as the elevator doors closed.

Huh? *That was weird. How did she know my name?* I didn't have time to think about that, though, as I hustled left, then right, and then to the science room.

When I finally flung open the door, the class was already in session, and who do you think was sitting right in the front row, center?

Yup. Blair, in all her glory. *Thanks for helping the new girl,* I thought.

She smirked as I sank into the nearest seat.

Lunchtime can be hard even when you're at a school with your best friends. If you come at the wrong moment, the line can be so long that your friends are finished by the time you sit down with your food. A bunch of dumb boys might nab the table you like by the window so that you have to sit with the younger kids somewhere. Sometimes the food can be awful. But nothing, nothing is worse than the feeling of standing with a full tray and having absolutely no one to sit with.

Standing with my iced tea, a steaming bowl of fresh ramen noodles, and a side of kimchi on my tray (the food options were way better here than at my old school), I surveyed the terrain. To my left were the younger kids: noisy, messy, not my speed. To my right were the older kids: cool, quiet, boys sitting with girls. Straight ahead, the kids seemed to be my age—boys still sat with boys, and girls with girls—but the tables were packed. The only possible spot was near Blair and a bunch of her friends, and there was no way I was making that mistake again.

Way in the back by the garbage bins was a half-empty table: social Siberia. I trudged toward it, not looking up; I didn't want to make eye contact with anyone, especially those girls. I set my tray down on the table and lifted my messenger bag off my shoulder, then sat and pulled out my phone. Never had I missed Tamiko and Sierra more than right then, not even when I'd been at camp for seven weeks.

I snapped a picture of my lunch tray and sent it to them, captioning it, Jealous? but what I really wanted to do was snap a pic of myself all alone at the table and send it to them with a caption saying, I miss you guys so much, it's taking all my willpower not to cry my eyes out right now.

I pressed send and began to eat, awaiting a reply. A minute passed, then two, and then I saw that they'd read it. I waited for a peppy reply, at least from Tamiko, who's super-quick on her phone, but nothing came. After another minute I felt worse than before. Were they also at lunch? Were they missing me too? Or had they already made a new friend to replace me?

The food was tasty, and without anyone to talk to, I finished quickly. I still had twenty-five minutes until my next class, and I couldn't sit there by myself and scroll through my phone the entire time; I'd be a sitting duck, just waiting to be picked on in some new way by the mean girls. So I gathered up my things, dealt with the unfamiliar trash/recycling/compost bins, and ditched my tray.

Back out in the hall, I didn't know where else to go, so I decided to head to my usual happy place: the library.

At least I knew where it was.

CHAPTER THREE
IRONY

The Vista Green library was a really beautiful space, and I knew I'd spend a lot of time there. I was looking forward to seeing Mrs. K. again—the only friendly (if somewhat odd) person I'd met so far that day. Back at my old school, Martin Luther King Middle, the librarian had been my favorite teacher, and she was the faculty member in charge of Book Fest, so we'd spent a lot of fun time together, planning and working on the event. Maybe Vista Green had something like Book Fest that I could get involved in; I'd ask Mrs. K.

The door swung open silently. There were a few students at computers at the desks, and even more spread around the back of the room, which opened out to a garden with lounge chairs. Around the room there were beanbag chairs and a few armchairs, and even a sofa, plus a rack of magazines and newspapers, and then rows and rows of books on the shelves beyond. There was a big desk area to my left, which was obviously Mrs. K.'s, and just to the right of it a massive fish tank was set into the wall. I let out a sigh of happiness. This could be my new happy place.

Mrs. K. emerged from the stacks and seemed utterly unsurprised to find me standing in front of her again. She strode across the open area to her desk and surveyed me quickly from head to toe.

"Allie. Allie Shear. A reader. Come. Shelve these books for me, please." She nudged a cart full of books toward me.

"I . . . uh . . . okay." It was so weird how she knew who I was. And how did she know I liked to read? I'd barely said two words to her. Did the school distribute the new kids' files to every staff member here?

Mrs. K. paused for a brief moment, tiny hands on tiny hips, and looked me in the eye. "You *do* know the Dewey decimal system, don't you?"

"Yes!" My brain suddenly sprang to life. I ditched my messenger back next to her desk and pushed the cart toward the bookshelves, grateful to have a place

39

to be and something to do for the next twenty-two minutes.

I felt happy and safe as I shelved the books, confidently locating their homes, and saying hi to my favorite books as I passed them. It was like seeing old friends. Plus, I spotted lots of appealing new books as I worked. *Okay,* I thought. *So I won't have any human friends here, if today was any indication. At least I can have books as friends.*

Pretty soon the cart was empty and I had a few minutes left to get to my next class. I finally felt like myself as I wheeled the cart back to the front of the library and Mrs. K.'s desk, only to find my messenger bag splayed open on the floor and *Anne of Green Gables* lying out in the open on the sage carpet. Worse, Blair was standing over it, snickering.

My jaw dropped and my face flushed with heat as I tried to think of what to do or say. But suddenly Mrs. K. was there, taking the cart from me and giving a withering stare to the mean girls.

"Blair! Maria! Palmer! Don't just stand there. If you knock something over, you must pick it right up!"

Shockingly, they did just as she'd said, putting the book and my phone back into the bag and handing my bag to me sheepishly.

"Sorry," whispered Maria, with the long white-blond hair. She didn't look sorry, though.

I glanced around, and I could see all the kids in the area watching us. I nodded.

Mrs. K. continued. "Excellent choice of reading material, Allie. Nothing like a classic, and right on trend. I suppose you've seen all the film adaptations of the Anne series, including the latest, which is *very* stylish and, I must say, quite well done, though really for teens, not middle schoolers. You must have quite sophisticated taste. Okay. Now, girls, don't let me see you hanging around here again with nothing to do, or I'll put you to work. Now, Allie, where to next, you? Upstairs? Hmmm?"

The girls scuttled off while Mrs. K. yammered on, but I was still standing there in shock at how quickly she'd defused the situation and sent the mean girls packing. I let her give me directions to my math room, and then I stumbled out the door like a zombie from Tanner's new favorite show, *The Walking Zombie Toads* (which is totally gross and inappropriate, as usual).

On the stairs I had a bit of a delayed reaction to

the bag incident, and I felt tears well. Why were these girls so mean? But just as quickly I channeled Anne Shirley and made myself focus on the limitless possibilities of Mrs. K. and the library.

Mrs. K. was a little odd, but at least she seemed to know me, and she had already helped me twice today. Plus she obviously loved books, and her library was awesome.

I survived the first day and lived to tell the tale. It wasn't a good day, but I guess it wasn't a total disaster. At home Tanner was filled with rambling stories of his new school and how he had two best friends, and the teacher had said he was so smart, and their classroom had a pet guinea pig. My mom beamed in satisfaction at him. But whenever she looked at me, her face would cloud over. I was always the happy student in the family, and Tanner was always fighting against school. It was pretty funny to see him as the happy student now, and me as the miserable one. My old English teacher, Mr. Campbell, would have called that "ironic."

Finally my mom interrupted Tanner's story of the ketchup at lunch, saying, "Hey! Do you guys want to come see the progress we've made on the store?"

"Like, now?" asked Tanner.

Usually we went to buy the rest of our school supplies on the first day of school. I guess everything was changing.

"Sure," I said, though all I really wanted to do was go lie on my new bed with Diana and lose myself in a good book. I couldn't face calling Tamiko or Sierra yet to see how their first day had gone, and I really didn't want to tell them about mine.

We walked to the store—it was only five blocks from our new house, and close enough to the beach for us to hear seagulls and feel a cool breeze. My mood lifted as the temperature dropped a little, and soon we reached the store.

The last time I had seen the store, it had been just an empty white box. "Okay, are you ready? Close your eyes," my mom instructed as we rounded the corner. She reached for our hands, and though I felt stupid walking down the street with my eyes closed, my hand in my mom's, I let her lead me. She brought us to the front of the store and then said, "Open!"

I opened my eyes and gasped. It was beautiful!

Outside hung a pale-blue-and-cream striped

awning, and the big plate-glass window said MOLLY'S
ICE CREAM in fat and swoopy gold lettering. Molly
was the name of my mom's grandmother, who'd
taught my mom how to make ice cream.

"Wow!" I said. "Does Grandma know?"

"Uh-huh," said my mom, grinning. "Now go in!"

Inside there was a tall, white-painted wooden
counter to my left for the cash register, with a built-in
organizer on the side for, I guessed, spoons and straws
and things like that. Behind the counter hung a white
painted sign that said MENU in fancy black script.
There were slots where flavor names could slide in,
and lists of drinks, some I'd never even heard of. (I
knew what a root beer float was, but an egg cream?
A lime rickey?)

Straight ahead were two long freezers with curved
glass case tops and enough bins for twelve ice cream
flavors. To the right of that were little buckets set into
the counter for toppings, with a slab of marble behind
it for creating mix-ins.

Behind the freezers was a wall of open shelves,
and above that were vintage metal letters with light
bulbs in them that spelled out ICE CREAM, like from
an old-fashioned carnival. A counter ran along the

back with electrical outlets in it (for milkshake blend-
ers and hot fudge warmers?), and at the far right was
a tall glass freezer with a door that swung open.

The store's floor was laid in tiny black and white
square tiles with flecks of gold in them, and the wall
to the far right was a giant mirror; past that was a little
hall with a bathroom and a closet. Up in front was a
high counter with stools looking out the window, and
three white-marble-topped tables with fancy curved
wire chairs around them. The puffy chair cushions
were done in plastic fabric that was the same as the
awning outside: blue and cream stripes.

The light fixtures hung from the ceiling at all different heights, and above the register was a cluster of
individual light bulbs hanging from cords; the bulbs
had been fitted with ceramic cones above them so
that it looked like a cluster of ice cream cones hanging upside down.

I couldn't believe it.

"*Wow*, Mom! This is awesome! It's like one of
those makeover shows on TV, where they do everything really fast!"

"Where's all the candy and ice cream?" asked
Tanner, looking around anxiously.

My mom laughed. "Excellent question. I have a big shipment coming in tomorrow, and then I have some ice cream in deep freeze storage at the industrial kitchen where I rent space. There's actually a little kitchen in the back here, where I can hand-make small batches of ice cream, and also bake the mix-ins, like marshmallow treats and pie. I'll probably have one or two fresh flavors of the day at any time, and then make the standard flavors in big batches at the industrial kitchen and bring them in as needed."

I was really impressed. It seemed like she'd been working on this for years, not just months. Maybe she had, if only in her imagination. I looked at my mom closely; she was like a different person in here—confident, upbeat, happy! It was kind of hard to believe she used to sit behind a desk looking at numbers all day and now she was going to scoop ice cream. I reached over and gave her a sideways hug.

"I'm so happy for you, Mama," I said, using my baby name for her.

She put her arms around me and Tanner (Tanner tried to squirm out, of course) and sighed happily, saying, "It's going to be better than great." Then she kissed each of us on our heads and gave one more squeeze before releasing us.

I glanced out the window and saw a group of girls about my age walking by. I didn't want to know if any of them were the mean girls.

Quickly I turned back toward my mom.

"Yes. We're going to be better than great," I agreed. But I crossed my fingers for courage as I said it.

CHAPTER FOUR

BOOK CLUB

Tamiko, Sierra, and I had a lot to say that first evening after school. My heart pinched as we video-chatted—they were together after carpooling home—and I missed them so much. Tamiko was wearing one of her usual eclectic outfits: a painted T-shirt with a bedazzled vest and a high ponytail sprouting out of the top of her head. Sierra looked soft and pretty in a loose-fitting romper. They were full of funny stories about kids we knew. Like, Jim Beatty had grown a mustache over the summer (it didn't look intentional), Lori Chambers had grown nearly a foot taller, and Jamie Hansen was dating a high schooler who might or might not ride a motorcycle. There was a new head lunch lady, and the food might have gotten marginally better.

I told them about the food at Vista Green, and how new and pretty the school was, and about kooky Mrs. K. If they noticed that I didn't mention any kids, they didn't let on, luckily. I tried to stay upbeat because I knew if I started to complain, I'd end up in tears, and I didn't want to go there just yet.

"We miss you, Allie Shear!" said Tamiko. "When are we going to see you?"

I sighed. "Maybe after school one day? Could we get together?"

Tamiko nodded. "I bet I could have my mom bring us over to your house one day this week."

My heart soared. "That would be so amazing."

As we were getting ready to hang up, Sierra smacked her forehead and said, "Oh, Allie, by the way, I'm going to need your help! Mrs. Olson was desperate for someone to help with Book Fest since you left, so I volunteered. I have no idea what I'm doing!"

My heart sank. Not only had my best friend taken over my old, beloved job, but she didn't even like to read! Plus she was always totally disorganized and overcommitted! Book Fest was in trouble, and there was not much I could do about it except grit my teeth and say, "Happy to help, anytime."

My second day of school was a little better than my first. For one thing, Tamiko and Sierra had texted our group chat to say they could come over after school. Knowing I was seeing my friends kept a little flame of happiness burning in my heart all day. For another thing, I knew my way around the building a little better, so I didn't feel like a total alien. And finally, I didn't waste any time at lunch but quickly ate my bánh mì sandwich and ran straight down to the library. Mrs. K. was at her desk and said, "Yes. Good. Okay. Mmm-hmm. Here they are, all ready for you," as I walked in.

I always felt like Mrs. K. was mid-conversation with me whenever I saw her—like we'd already established something, but I was never sure what. Being with Mrs. K. was like reading a book that took place entirely in the present, and you had to figure out the backstory as you went along—confusing but also kind of intriguing.

Today she handed me a stack of flyers to deliver to every teacher around the school, not really asking me to do it but proceeding as if I'd already agreed to whatever it was. I had to laugh a little, she was so funny with her run-on monologues and her chic outfits. (Today: a caramel-colored wrap dress with caramel-colored slingbacks—*click, click, click*—and a chunky necklace of smooth wooden links.) I scooped up the pile of flyers from her and began walking, classroom to classroom, to hand them to the teachers or leave them on their desks.

I wasn't sure if I should look at the flyers or not, since they were for the teachers, but after a few empty classrooms (all the teachers were at lunch), I decided that Mrs. K. wouldn't have given them to me to distribute if they'd been private. So I ducked into an alcove to read what the flyer said. It was a questionnaire, and Mrs. K. was looking for teachers to each fill one in and return it.

The questions were:

- Would you prefer an author visit or a book fair?
- Would you participate in an all-school read?
- Would you prefer that we emphasize fiction or nonfiction?
- Do the kids in your classes read independently? Do you?

My heart leapt at the words "book" and "fair" in the same sentence. Book Fest had been my absolute favorite thing at my old school. It was a three-day-long book fair with piles of books for sale on tables, where kids could stock up on their independent reading books for the year or learn about new books that their favorite authors had written. Sometimes authors or artists would come talk to us about writing or about the characters in the books. It would take over our lunchroom for the three days it ran, and we'd get to bring brown-bag lunches and eat at our desks. Each grade would get a shopping slot, and when it was our turn, we'd swarm the tables and make the tough decisions on how to spend the money we'd brought. Sometimes authors came and signed their books after we bought them. Best of all, we were allowed a free half hour of reading in our classroom every day during Book Fest.

My favorite times were once, in fifth grade, when my mom gave me the money to buy the *Anne of Green Gables* boxed set of beautiful flowered hardcovers and put it away for my birthday. The other was when I met a real live author of some books I'd read and she signed a book for me. She told me I could be an author too, but not in that kind of way adults sometimes do. She said it like I could really do it.

This year I was supposed to be in charge of all the student volunteers, and I was going to be the most senior student involved. I was also going to help the little kids make their book selections, which is something I would have loved. The librarian, Mrs. Olson, was going to let me have a lot of responsibility in running Book Fest this year, and I'd been looking forward to it all summer. Now I wouldn't even get to go.

But if we could have a book fair here at Vista Green, I could help, just like I had at my old school! I rushed to deliver the flyers all around, and if I met a teacher, I talked up the book fair idea. In about twenty minutes I had finished, and I raced back to the library to get my messenger bag. My next class was English—right next door to the library—and I was excited and nervous. English was always my favorite class.

I swooped into the library. Mrs. K. was at her desk. She was busy looking at something on her computer. It was funny how she never thanked me for my help, but I didn't mind. I struggled with whether or not to say something about a book fair—mentioning it would reveal that I'd read the flyers—but how could

I not, given my background and experience?

"Oh, Mrs. K.! I hope we get to have a book fair! It would be so wonderful! At my old school—"

"Pish-posh!" said Mrs. K., spinning in her chair to face me. "We don't need a book fair! Book fairs are crass and commercial. They have to do with shopping, not reading. Some schools sell *trinkets* at their book fairs. And *dolls!*" She shivered dramatically. "Give me a well-read, well-loved copy of an old book any day. I'd like an all-school read, but the teachers don't want the extra work. We'll see about that. Yes. Mmm-hmm. Okay." She spun her chair back around to her computer and was clearly finished with me for the day.

I stood there, stunned, for an extra second. I felt as if I'd been slapped in the face. All my enthusiasm drained out of me and I turned to slink out the door.

Was I wrong for loving Book Fest? So what if they sold trinkets and toys? They brought people in to look at the books. And wasn't that what Book Fest was all about?

I turned left toward the classroom for my first English class. I did not have high hopes. I felt totally out of sync with the only book lover I had met so far at my new school.

Ms. Healy was the name of my new English teacher, and I fervently hoped we would be in sync—*kindred spirits*, as Anne Shirley would have said. I entered Ms. Healy's classroom cautiously, but I hadn't needed to be nervous. The kids were all milling around, some sitting on Ms. Healy's desk, legs swinging happily as they chatted with her. Ms. Healy was young, with thick blond hair that fell to her shoulders, like a girl in a shampoo commercial, and with apple cheeks and sparkling blue eyes. She kind of looked like a kid herself, as she was wearing a cute pink-and-white dress I'd admired recently at the mall.

There were beanbag chairs in the back of the classroom, and there was a whole wall of low bookshelves packed with books. Along the top of the bookshelves were huge stacks of paper and colorful jars of pens of every kind. The bulletin boards on the two walls were papered in bright hues but blank, waiting for our work, I guessed. Along another wall was a display. It said: THE MUSEUM OF THE WRITTEN WORD: SOME OF ITS MANY USES. And there were a bunch of DVDs under a sign that said SCREENWRITING, then a bunch of grocery store products with a sign saying

MARKETING, ADVERTISING, PROMOTIONAL WRITING. Next was a stack of newspapers and magazines with a sign that said JOURNALISM, and finally there were some old cell phones in a pile under a sign that said SOCIAL MEDIA. All around the border of the classroom, next to the ceiling, were portraits of famous writers with their names underneath them, like a gallery. There was everyone from Gary Paulsen and Beverly Cleary to Jane Austen and Alice Walker.

Hmm, I thought, cautiously optimistic. *This is pretty cool.*

Suddenly Ms. Healy called, "Colin, the lights, please!" and a kid jumped up and turned off all the lights. *What on earth?* I thought. *Should I be scared?* I looked around. None of the other kids seemed nervous. It was like they knew what was coming.

Then Ms. Healy switched on a spotlight at her desk. The spotlight shone up onto a disco ball hanging from the ceiling, and loud pop music came blaring out of a speaker. I stood, speechless, as all the kids jumped up—onto desks, chairs, anything—and began dancing. Ms. Healy danced her way over to me and spoke loudly over the music. "Hi, Allie! Welcome to our class! We like to get our creative juices flowing with our disco minute at the start of every class." She led me to a desk in the middle of everyone. "Here's your seat. Enjoy!" Then she danced away, back to her desk.

I stood and looked around in wonder, bobbing a little to the beat, feeling self-conscious but liking what I saw. Sure enough, when the minute was over, Colin flipped the overhead lights back on, Ms. Healy silenced the music and switched off the spotlight, and everyone sat down, smiling.

I knew I had just found my favorite teacher at Vista Green.

"Okay, and then, the room has beanbags, and there was a disco minute, and Ms. Healy is much more fun than Mrs. K., who I'd *thought* was going to be my favorite. And maybe they're *both* my favorite, but . . ."

Tamiko and Sierra were over at my house, and I was filling them in on everything. It felt weird for them to not know who I was talking about, or be able to picture the layout of the school. I promised to snap some pics on my phone or take a little video of it and e-mail it to them.

"Do they give you a lot of homework?" Sierra asked, eyebrows knit together.

57

I smiled. Sierra absolutely hated homework, but I think it was because she always left it till the last minute and then forgot to bring home the reading, or softball practice would run late, or the star of the play would get sick and she'd be the understudy and have to learn all the lines. It was always some drama with her and homework. "I can't tell yet. I have a ton of reading—"

Tamiko waved her hand in the air and made a "Pffft!" noise. "Oh, please. Reading isn't work for you. It's like breathing. You're gonna do it anyway! Your whole life is like one long book club." She flicked her long, dark side ponytail over her shoulder and scoffed again.

I grinned and reached over for a hug, but Tamiko batted me away, as always. "Oh, stop with your fancy hugs. You know I hate that stuff!"

"And that's why we love you!" cried Sierra, which was our cue to dive onto Tamiko and grab her in a big group hug.

We spilled off my bed onto the floor, laughing. It was such a relief to be with my friends again, people who knew me and got me and liked me. I had felt like an alien on another planet these past two days—like an invisible person, or worse, depending on who was around. Tamiko and Sierra always made me feel better.

I hadn't yet told Sierra and Tamiko about the mean girls at Vista Green. Partly because it was so humiliating that I thought I might cry in the retelling, and partly because Tamiko would want immediate revenge, and I wasn't up for that negative energy right now.

"So do you guys want to come see the store, or what?" I asked, bouncing in place.

"Yes! Let's go! I'm dying to see it!" said Tamiko, hopping up. Tamiko was all about the *new*. She was always on these wild websites looking for new trends and following foreign fashion accounts that her cousins in Japan told her about, and building inspiration boards with clips of her latest obsessions. Everything was a blank slate for Tamiko, just waiting for her imagination to roar into gear and tweak, decorate, redo, enhance, and make it unique. I couldn't wait to see what she thought of Molly's Ice Cream. It was pretty great as it was, but she just might have some ideas on how to make it even better.

We walked to the store, the blocks whizzing past as we chatted a mile a minute. Being with them was like drinking a cool milkshake after a long, dry thirst. Sierra was filling us in on her twin sister Isabel's soccer triumphs, and Tamiko told us about her brother Kai's latest entrepreneurial scheme to sell hurricane survival packs door to door. (We got hit by bad hurricanes almost every year.) There wasn't much for me to tell about Tanner (who wants to hear about burps and stinky sneakers?), so we quickly ended up on the topic of my parents, which is where I think we were headed anyway.

I'd told them both the news by text after I had woken up and realized that it wasn't all a bad dream. Sierra had replied immediately, her text filled with emojis of sad faces and hearts and "I love you." Tamiko didn't respond for about half an hour, and when she did, it was with one bracingly simple word: Good.

It actually shocked me into laughter when I saw it, because for goodness' sake, she was right! It *was* good that they were getting divorced. My parents seemed so much happier already, and I felt so much gratitude to Tamiko in that moment for looking beyond the obvious reaction to the true reaction. But just because my parents were happier didn't necessarily mean *I* was happier.

"So, how's it going with, you know . . . ," began Sierra, gentle and considerate, as always.

"The big split," said Tamiko, always one to just rip off the bandage and take the pain as it came.

"It's weird," I said, relieved to talk about it. I'd been thinking in advance about what I'd tell them, because I knew they'd ask, and I wanted to answer as truthfully as possible. "I think with all the changes happening at once, it's sort of good because it's distracting. And then on top of it, they're both so crazy happy, like *relieved*, that it's kind of contagious. And then there's the store, which will be great," I added.

Tamiko looked at me and raised an eyebrow. "Okay. It's good for them. How about you?"

Sierra looked at me expectantly. I was trying to be brave, but these girls knew me too well. "It's hard," I said softly. "It's weird and hard and, well, just a lot to process."

Sierra gave me a squeeze.

"They keep telling us that this is going to be better," I said.

"Well, you just have to trust that it is," said Sierra.

"Well, it might not be," said Tamiko, and Sierra shot her a look. "I mean, new house, new school, you don't see your dad as much. That's a lot to deal with."

"Tamiko!" Sierra scolded.

"No," I said, laughing. "She's right. It's a lot. A whole lot."

"But your parents were really miserable together," said Tamiko. "So I do think it will be better."

"Well, I don't know about 'miserable,'" I said.

"Oh, yes," said Tamiko. "They were miserable. I mean, they fought all the time. They couldn't stand to be in the same room together!"

"TAMIKO!" shouted Sierra.

"What?" said Tamiko. "It's totally true! I can't believe you didn't see that, Allie."

"I saw it," I said. "But it's a different thing to process when it's your own parents."

Everyone was quiet as we rounded the corner.

"You're right," said Tamiko. "I'm sorry. It's not like it's just anyone's parents. They're your parents."

"It's okay," I said. "It's good to talk about it a little."

Sierra flung her arm around me. "Okay, now let's talk ice cream."

"Close your eyes and give me your hands," I directed, mimicking my mom.

I led them to the edge of the curb in front of the store. Then I said, "Voilà!"

CHAPTER FIVE

CHARACTER DEVELOPMENT

Sierra gasped and lifted her hands to her mouth. She clasped them there and shook her head slowly in wonder. Tamiko laughed out loud and turned to high-five me.

"Wow!" she said appreciatively. "Talk about curb appeal!"

"Pretty cool, huh? Do you like it?" I asked, but I couldn't hide my grin; I could already tell they loved it.

"Cool? I'm moving in. Now get out of my way!" Tamiko pushed me aside and entered the store, and a new little bell tinkled above the door.

My mom was inside, and she came out from the back at the sound of the bell, wiping her hands on her apron.

"Girls!" she cried, holding her arms wide. My mom loves my besties, which makes me so happy. She always tells me that if she were my age, she'd pick them as her friends too.

Tamiko and Sierra ran to embrace her, squealing and jumping up and down in excitement.

"Mrs. S.! This rocks!" said Tamiko, turning in place to take it all in.

"Are you so excited? It's your lifelong dream come true!" said Sierra.

My mom was beaming. "I *am* so excited. And thank you for your enthusiasm. Now come into the back and try my new flavor. It's cinnamon ice cream with crumbled lace butter cookies in it."

"Yum!" said Sierra.

We trailed my mom into the back, and she doled out samples of her new flavor while we chatted.

"Oh, Allie, Mrs. Olson says hi and she misses you," said Sierra. "We had a planning meeting for Book Fest, and she kept mentioning you."

My smile faded. "Bummer. Tell her I say hi back. I miss her, too."

"Yeah, well, we're really understaffed this year," said Sierra, shaking her head regretfully. "And I have so much going on, with the can drive for Thanksgiving, and student council, and dance, plus the newspaper...."

I had to crack a smile at her laundry list of activities. Sierra always overcommitted herself and then had a hard time delivering. Inside, I cringed a little to think of it being her instead of me helping Mrs. Olson with Book Fest.

"Hey! I know. You should ask MacKenzie to help you!" said Tamiko.

"Oh! That's a great idea!" Sierra turned to me. "MacKenzie is this new girl. She's super-nice. You'd really like her, Allie. We've told her all about you. You two definitely need to meet!" said Sierra, nodding enthusiastically.

Tamiko turned to me. "Yeah, she's in all our classes, so we've gotten to know her pretty fast. You'll love her."

"Great," I said weakly. I could feel my mom watching me, but I refused to meet her eye. I couldn't help but feel it was her fault that I didn't get to go to school with my best friends anymore, and her fault that I didn't know this new girl. No one had tried to be friends with me at the new school. There was only

Blair and her band of mean girls trying to send me to the nonexistent pool.

"Oh, Allie! Guess what else! I can't believe I forgot to tell you. I've already told everyone else I know, so I guess it feels like old news, but Maya Burns is coming to sign her books at Book Fest this year!"

My jaw dropped. "Maya Burns? Seriously? She's only my second-favorite author, after—"

"Lucy Maud Montgomery!" singsonged Tamiko and Sierra. They love to tease me about my *Anne of Green Gables* obsession.

"I know!" added Sierra. "Maybe I can get her to sign a book for you!"

"Yeah," I said, feeling deflated. My best friends would get to meet my second-favorite author, and I wouldn't, and they didn't really even care about books!

Tamiko's phone pinged. "Oh, that's MacKenzie now." She read the snap and laughed. "She sent a funny photo, but she just wants to know what the homework is for math." Tamiko consulted her notes, then typed back quickly, her thumbs a blur on the screen.

"Anyway," said Sierra, sensing that Tamiko's behavior was a little rude. "Tell me more about your plans for the store, Mrs. Shear. It's so amazing already."

I suddenly wondered if my mom would continue to go by "Mrs. Shear." It would be weird for my friends to call her anything else. I mean, they couldn't really call her "Meg" like *her* friends did, could they? Was she going to go back to her maiden name? There were so many things I just didn't know right now. I glanced at my mom. I'd have to ask her about all this later.

Mom chatted about the shop and led the girls back out to the front to point out a few things.

"You should get one of those customized photo frames, so people can hold it in front of them and snap pics to post on social media," suggested Tamiko. "Also, make sure to register your business name and GPS so people can tag it in posts. And you might want to consider purchasing a filter. You know, like the one where people's faces turn into dogs, but maybe instead of puppy ears, they get ice cream cone hats!"

"Good ideas!" said my mom admiringly. She pulled a small notebook out of her pocket and wrote down Tamiko's suggestions.

"Will you do mail order?" asked Tamiko. "And

what about flavor of the day or month? That's so big on social media."

While Tamiko and my mom were devising marketing strategies, Sierra and I sat down on stools at the window-front counter to chat.

"I miss you guys," I said.

"We miss you so much, *chica*!" said Sierra, her eyes misting. She reached over and hugged me hard. "But we can still see each other a lot, like this."

I shook my head. "I think it's going to be hard to fit in, once homework ramps up and the school year gets going. I wish we did some activity together, like soccer or ballet, where it was a guarantee that we'd see each other every week."

"Yeah," agreed Sierra, lost in thought.

Tamiko arrived at our side. "MacKenzie thinks it's so cool that your mom owns an ice cream store. I told her to come by."

"What, *now*?" I said. I had thought this was our time to be together—you know, the three of us, just like it used to be.

"Yeah! She's super-cool. You're going to love her. I can't wait—"

"Tamiko!" said Sierra sharply. "*No.* This is *our* time

with Allie. Tell MacKenzie maybe another day."

"What?" Tamiko looked confused. But then comprehension washed over her face. "Oh! Right. Oh, I'm sorry, Allie. I wasn't thinking. You're right. Hang on." Her fingers flew over her keyboard as her dark eyes narrowed in concentration. "Okay. Done. Sorry. That wasn't very sensitive of me." She patted me on the head. "Sorry, little one."

We all laughed, because I was about three inches taller than Tamiko.

One of the things I loved most about Tamiko was that there was never any drama, never any beating around the bush. She was so direct that little upsets didn't have time to fester and become big problems.

"Anyway, *someday* you'll meet MacKenzie, *if* we're even still friends with her, and then you *might* like her. That's all! Now, what are we going to do this weekend?" Tamiko grinned.

"Something fun," I said.

Soon we were planning what to do on Saturday— movies, mall, maybe lie out by the beach. By the time I got home that evening, I felt much better— reconnected to my friends, and with something to look forward to for the weekend.

On the bus the next morning, I headed straight to the back. But halfway down the aisle, Colin from my English class looked up from the newspaper he was reading. "Hey! Allie. Here." He patted the seat next to him as he scooted toward the window.

I had an urge to look over my shoulder to make sure it was me he was really talking to (as if there might be another Allie standing behind me), but I decided the better part of being cool was just *acting* cool, so I smiled and joined him.

"Hi," he said. "I'm Colin. From English class."

I nodded. "I know. You do a mean light switch."

He smiled. "Thanks. I was new last year too. Came in at the middle of the year. It stinks at first, but then it gets suddenly much better. I couldn't watch the girls torture you again this morning."

I grinned. "So you saw that?"

"I didn't even need to see. But don't worry, no one really pays attention to them. There are nice kids in the grade too. I'll introduce you."

"Cool," I said, and we chatted the whole rest of the way to school. Colin was the assistant editor of the school paper, hoping to run it next year, and he told me all about it on the ride. Like me, he loved to read and write, and English was his favorite subject. He confirmed my feelings about Ms. Healy (she was awesome, and everyone was desperate to be in her class), and Mrs. K. (a little kooky but smart and very nice and interesting).

As the bus pulled in and we shuffled off, Colin said, "See you in English!" and I knew I'd just made my first friend at Vista Green—a kindred spirit.

At lunch I sat with Colin, and he introduced me to two nice girls, as promised. Amanda and Eloise were both in my grade, and we connected well, even if they weren't immediate replacements for Sierra and Tamiko. It's hard for new friends to compete with friends you've had since you were a toddler.

I didn't want to overstay my welcome, so I ate pretty quickly and then excused myself. I was curious to see if Mrs. K. had gotten any results in from her survey, so I headed down to check in.

In the library Ms. Healy and Mrs. K. were chatting at Mrs. K.'s desk, and they both looked happy to see me.

I guess I must have looked a little anxious, because Ms. Healy jumped in immediately.

"We were just discussing some of the literacy initiatives for the year," said Ms. Healy. I knew that "literacy initiatives" meant "reading events and projects."

I looked at Mrs. K. "Any feedback on your surveys?" I privately hoped that there would be such an overwhelming vote for a book fair that she would have to cave. And then I could help her organize and run the whole thing! And we could call it Book Fest!

Mrs. K. hemmed and hawed and shuffled papers around on her desk as I waited for an answer.

"I'm a big fan of the all-school read," said Ms. Healy. "It would be wonderful to build some programming around the book's topic and have some guest speakers come in. My friend Ellen teaches over at Saint Joseph's High School and said her school read a nonfiction crime book. The school had the mayor and the chief of police read it, and then they came in and met with the students. Each teacher had to prepare two classes around the book, so Ellen, being a science teacher, did a class on forensics and evidence and crime scene contamination. She even had a teacher friend barge in and out during the class, and then she quizzed kids on their eyewitness descriptions of the woman, to see how observant they were."

"Cool!" I said. "Just like on TV!"

"Hmm, yes, very interesting," agreed Mrs. K., nodding her head enthusiastically.

"There are a million things you could do. I get excited just thinking about it!" I gushed.

Ms. Healy smiled at me. "Maybe we need to form a committee, with student advisors. . . ."

My heart leapt! This was just what I'd been hoping! Maybe I'd get to help run a book fair after all.

But she continued. "We might not be able to organize something for this year, but we could get ready for next year."

Inwardly I groaned. A whole year? Outwardly I continued to nod and said I'd love to help.

Mrs. K. was biting her lip thoughtfully as she gathered the stack of surveys and shook and tapped them into a neat pile. "The surveys are saying book fair." She rolled her eyes.

My heart leapt again, but I played it cool. "I'd help with that! I mean, if you did it. I love book fairs."

"Maybe we could do a book fair off-site on a

weekend?" suggested Ms. Healy. "Or join forces with another school, or even the town library. Make it a fund-raiser?"

Mrs. K. hammered away on her keyboard, finished with the conversation for now and ignoring us. Ms. Healy winked at me. "You're on our steering committee now, anyway. We'll figure something out. We've got a budget for something."

The chimes sounded, and Ms. Healy and I walked to her classroom together.

When I got home at dinnertime, I had a whole series of snaps from Tamiko with suggestions for the ice cream shop, and a few from Sierra, asking what she should wear to the grand opening of the store this Sunday. I also had friend requests from Colin, Amanda, and Eloise, all of which I accepted. Things were looking up!

Just before bed I got one last snap from Tamiko. It said, Can I bring MacKenzie to the opening on Sunday?

My heart sank. *This again?* As I was mulling over my reply, Tamiko pinged me once more.

Kidding! it said, and I laughed out loud.

CHAPTER SIX
SETTING

This weekend was my and Tanner's first weekend to spend with our dad, and it all went pretty well. He burned the hamburgers on Friday night because he wasn't used to cooking them on a stove instead of a grill, but it didn't matter because we cut them in half and scooped out and ate the middles dunked in ketchup. Then we ran upstairs to try the rooftop pool.

Let me tell you, when you are used to being at ground level, or maybe on a second or third floor, and suddenly you get the chance to be seven stories up, it is pretty eye-opening. The whole town was spread out before me, and it felt like I was looking at a map from the end pages of a book, like *The Boxcar Children*, which was my favorite book when I was little. Tanner and I even mapped out where our old house was. Even better, the pool was awesome! It was outdoors, open to the night sky, and encircled by brand-new cushy white lounge chairs. There were bright yellow foam floats that anyone could use, and Tanner and I had a pirate war with ours (me stooping to his level, I admit) while my dad read the newspaper on a lounge chair.

But the best part was that while Tanner and I were resting between pirate bouts, Amanda from my class showed up with her younger sister. It turned out that her mom lived in this building too. We spent the rest of our time playing Marco Polo, all four of us in the pool, until it was dark and my fingertips were like raisins.

As we got off the elevator at my dad's floor, I invited Amanda and her sister, Maddy, to the ice cream shop opening on Sunday. Then I winced as I realized that I was having a double standard, since I hadn't wanted Tamiko to invite MacKenzie. So when I got back to my new room, I raced to my phone and snapped Sierra and Tamiko to say that they should bring MacKenzie if she wanted to come, and anyone else. The more the merrier, anyway!

Being at Dad's was fun, but it was kind of like we were away on a vacation without Mom, which was weird. Plus I wasn't used to being in an apartment. I could hear doors opening and closing and someone upstairs walking around. It was comforting to know that I was surrounded by people. Then I heard my door swing open.

"Allie?" It was Tanner.

"What's wrong?" I asked.

"I can't sleep," he said softly. "My room is scary."

"Scary?" I asked. "You mean just because it's new and everything is unfamiliar?"

"Yeah," he said. "I keep hearing footsteps."

"Come here," I said, scooting over and making room for him. He climbed in next to me and put his head on my shoulder. He hadn't done that in a long time.

"I want to go home," he said.

"To Mom's house?" I asked.

"No, *home*," Tanner said emphatically. "Our old house."

I sighed. I knew what he meant.

The light flicked on in the hall, and Dad peeked in. He looked worried for a second, but then smiled.

"You guys okay?" he asked.

"It's weird in my room," said Tanner.

"What's weird?" asked Dad. "The lights? Is your bed not comfortable?"

"It's just weird," said Tanner.

Dad sat down on the bed. "Well, this is new for all of us. We all have new rooms and new beds and new houses. It's a lot to get used to."

"Times two!" said Tanner. "New at Mom's house and new at your house."

"I know," said Dad softly. "I know, buddy. It's really weird for me to be in the apartment by myself when you guys aren't here. I miss you so much. But we're going to get through this together."

We were all quiet for a while.

"I have an idea," Dad said. "Who wants a midnight snack?"

"I do!" yelled Tanner, sitting up.

We followed Dad out to the kitchen. He opened a cabinet and looked a little guilty. "I, uh, got a few snacks for the new place."

He took out some chips and dips, then a bag of marshmallows.

"Dad!" I said, laughing. "That's quite a stockpile!"

Dad put everything on a plate and carried it out to the living room. We put on one of our favorite movies and all settled in.

"We can have a slumber party!" Dad said.

Tanner fell asleep pretty quickly lying on Dad. Then Dad fell asleep too. I thought for a minute about going into my room, but I put my head on Dad's shoulder and just snuggled in.

Saturday morning Dad took us to the batting cages and miniature golf, which was kind of a family tradition. It was weird to be there without Mom, and I think we were all feeling it. Dad kept saying, "This is our *new normal*," like it was some kind of spell he wanted to come true. We were all a little sad afterward, so when Dad suggested we stop by to see Mom at the ice cream store, we were all in favor.

At Molly's, Mom was all aflutter: accepting a delivery, painting part of the counter that had gotten dinged up by the dishwasher installation, talking on her cell phone to the health inspector about where to post her certificate, and baking some Saint Louis butter cake to try in a new ice cream flavor. She waved happily when she saw us and gratefully doled out a few tasks. I think we were all relieved to experience

79

the "old normal" for an hour and a half before my dad said it was time for lunch for him and Tanner.

Tamiko and Sierra wanted us all to go to the mall in the afternoon. I had felt funny about ditching Dad on his first weekend alone with us, but Mom had assured me it would be okay. She said it wasn't my job to entertain my parents; I just needed to go on living my life, and things would start to feel normal. (There was that word again! Ms. Healy would be asking me for an alternative word choice by now.) So I agreed to the plan.

Mrs. Sato was picking me up at Dad's at twelve thirty, and I was ready and downstairs by twelve twenty-five. Sure enough, at twelve twenty-nine their white SUV cruised up, and Tamiko rolled down the window and gave me the peace sign. It was always so funny to see her short mom driving around in such a big car. She practically had to take a running start down the driveway to get into it.

I hopped in and submitted to Mrs. Sato's grilling me about my new school all the way to the mall. She was envious that I got to go to Vista Green and said she was always looking for a house to move to so Tamiko and Kai could rezone to that school district.

"Imagine if I got to come to your school!" said Tamiko.

"Nooooo!" wailed Sierra. "Who would help me with all my assignments if you were both gone?"

"Hmm," I said, turning to Tamiko. "Maybe you *should* move to my school, and maybe then Little Miss Forgetful would start to take care of herself a tiny bit better!" I teased.

Sierra folded her arms across her chest and fake-pouted. "I just have a lot on my plate!" she said.

"That's because you always take extra helpings!" joked Tamiko.

Sierra made a scoffing noise. "I can't help it if I like to be involved."

"I think you need to start sitting on your hands in meetings so that you don't volunteer for anything else," I said. I felt a little mean saying it, but secretly I wished she hadn't volunteered to run Book Fest.

"I'll sit on them for you!" shouted Tamiko, scooching over toward Sierra, who shrieked.

"Here we are, kiddos!" announced Mrs. Sato as she pulled up in front of the Commons, which was our town's answer to a mall. It wasn't like the old-fashioned malls where everything was on multiple floors under one huge roof. Instead it was styled as a small village, and you had to be outdoors on these cool covered boardwalk-style sidewalks to go from store to store. We all loved it. There was one area that was all food trucks—this mall's version of a food court—and it had lots of seating under a huge shady tentlike canopy, and big outdoor air conditioners that blew mist over you to cool you off.

We hopped out of the car with promises to behave, and set a pickup time for four o'clock. Then we began the bargaining.

"Please, please—bookstore first!" I said.

"But you never even buy anything. All we do is go there for an hour and you visit the books you already own!" protested Sierra.

"That's not true! I buy a new book every month; I just like reading library books and eBooks, so I mix it up and don't spend all my money on one thing."

Tamiko said, "All I know is, I have to get to the arts and crafts store for some new sequins and yarn, and then the hardware store for a glue gun."

"I can only imagine what kind of project this is for. Are you customizing your toilet seat this week?" I teased.

"No, but *that* is a great idea! I need to search for ideas for that when I get home!" said Tamiko.

I groaned. "It was a joke!"

It felt great to be back with my besties doing one of our usual activities. We had a certain routine at the mall and certain things we liked to visit (the Wishing Fountain, the human-size chessboard, the Skee-Ball arcade, and the temporary-tattoo vending machine, to name a few), and of course, certain things we liked to eat, in certain orders. A lot of it was unspoken—we just settled into our usual pattern. The day was warm but not hot, and the sky was blue, and I was happier than I'd been since camp, practically skipping as we walked and joked.

We didn't do much before we were all starving and had to go to the Arepa Lady's truck. She made these delicious thick and chewy cornmeal pancakes filled with cheese that you could top with any kind of shredded meat (or not). We always started with her, and then went to the Belgian frites guy for french fries with sriracha mayo dipping sauce, and then the bubble tea guy for drinks. We'd finally completed gathering everything and were just turning to sit at a picnic table when there was a loud squeal from behind us. Everybody turned around.

"*Niñas!*" cried a voice.

"*Niña!*" Tamiko and Sierra called in excitement, hastily dropping all their things onto the table and turning quickly toward someone.

I carefully put my assorted things down onto the table and lifted a few of their things that had toppled over, then turned curiously to see who had called to us. I couldn't make out the person's face because the three of them were in a group hug, jumping up and down. But I could see that she had long, straight, bright red hair and wore very stylish white jeans with a thick white T-shirt, and on her feet, a pair of black sneakers with a shiny logo, which I knew were Tamiko's absolute favorite brand of sneaker. (Or at least they once were—her favorite seemed to change daily.) As they pulled apart from their little love fest, I looked at the girl's face and did not know her. My heart sank.

A new friend.

"*Niñas,*" they called one another. The three of us always called ourselves "*chicas.*"

The three of them stood chatting rapidly, and I wasn't sure what to do. I was standing there debating

84

whether to say something and idly eating french fries from the paper cone they'd come in, when I looked around to see who else was there, and suddenly my stomach dropped. The "Mean Team" was at a table across the tent, their eyes bouncing back and forth between me and the threesome. Now I was really doomed.

Standing there alone, I looked like the loser they already thought me to be. I wanted to shout, *"Those are my best friends over there!"* but the girls would have just laughed at me, because, come on, it sure didn't look like it.

But if I walked over to Tamiko, Sierra, and the other girl and they ignored me, left me standing on the outside, it would look even worse. My face grew red and my heart thudded as Maria leaned in to Blair and Palmer and whispered something that made them all giggle.

That was it! I had to act!

Quickly I marched across the open pavilion to the bubble tea truck to get an extra straw. I already had one, but I needed something to do with myself while I waited for my friends. I needed to look busy!

I passed as close as possible to Tamiko, Sierra, and

"*niña* girl," but none of them acknowledged me; they were all chatting away excitedly. I couldn't help it. Tears welled in my eyes and I bypassed the bubble tea guy and headed straight for the bathroom at the far end of the food area.

The tears spilled over just as I reached the door, but I held my head up and didn't cave until I'd reached the stall and locked the door behind me. Then I gave in to the silent, racking sobs I'd been fighting for what felt like forever. What was happening to me and my friends? It was all too much.

I blew my nose and patted my wet cheeks with some tissue. I stepped out of the stall and went to wash my face, and just as I reached the sink, Sierra appeared.

"Allie! There you are!" she cried in relief. "We were worried about you!"

She saw that I had been crying and rushed over. "Oh, Allie! What's wrong?"

I felt huffy. "It sure didn't seem like you noticed me," I muttered.

"Allie, that was MacKenzie! We wanted you to meet her. But Tamiko was scared after the other day that you'd be mad if we dragged her over to you. So we were waiting for you to come say hello, but then you blew us off. What happened to you?"

"Wait, *I* blew *you* off? You guys didn't even look at me once MacKenzie showed up! It was like I was invisible! And what's worse, the Mean Team was there. . . ."

Sierra paused. "Who?"

Uh-oh. I had deliberately not told Sierra and Tamiko about the mean girls because it was so embarrassing (and, as I mentioned before, I did not want Tamiko to start a rumble with them).

I sighed. "The three mean girls from my class who are always making fun of me. They were out there, and I got embarrassed at being left out, so I ran in here."

"Oh no!" said Sierra. "I'm so sorry! I didn't know there were mean girls in your class. Why didn't you tell us?"

I didn't want to cry again, so I said, "Can we just go eat? I'm sure all our food is cold by now, but I think I'd feel better if I ate. Then I can tell you everything, okay?"

Sierra looped her arm through mine. "Let's go, *chica.*"

We walked back to the table, and I saw the Mean Team looking at us. I must have been looking in that direction, because Sierra whispered, "Is that them?" as we walked by. I nodded a little, and she squeezed my hand.

When we got back to the table, Tamiko was blustering about where I had been, and how I'd missed MacKenzie, but Sierra just put her palm out in Tamiko's face like a traffic cop and said, "Wait. She's starving," so Tamiko waited.

I stole a glance across the tent as I wolfed down my arepa, and saw that the mean girls were gone, thankfully. By the time my stomach was full and I had taken a few deep breaths, I did feel much better. I told Sierra and Tamiko everything, and it felt so good to come clean and be totally honest with them. I realized I'd been sugarcoating everything, not wanting to look like I couldn't handle the changes, not wanting to look like I was a loser in my new school, and most of all, not wanting to look like I couldn't make it without them. The funny thing was, it was *I* who hadn't been treating *them* like my best friends.

As expected, Tamiko's face tightened and her fists balled as I told them about the bus and the phony directions to the science lab, the book bag "accidentally" dumped onto the library floor, the giggles in the lunchroom and under the tent today. But I redirected her by saying it really wouldn't help me at all if my friend from my old school was mean to kids from my new school. By then we'd cleaned up our lunch wrappers, sorted all the recycling, and headed back down Market Street toward the bookstore.

"I am so sorry you've been having a hard time without us," said Sierra, and I could see that her eyes were tearing up a little.

"Thanks," I said.

"Don't let anyone push you around, Allie. You're too nice," warned Tamiko.

I laughed. "You say that like it's a bad thing."

"Humph," said Tamiko.

We entered the bookstore to cheer me up, and my heart began to sing.

"Well, look who's here!" said Mrs. O'Brien, who owns the bookstore. "It's my Book Fest friend!"

Upon which I burst into tears again.

CHAPTER SEVEN
PACING

Sunday was hot and hazy. "A perfect day for selling ice cream!" declared my dad when he woke us up practically at dawn. Tanner and I shuffled to the table in our pj's to eat the oatmeal my dad had prepared. I know oatmeal isn't everyone's cup of tea, but the way my dad makes it—with hot maple syrup and a puddle of warm cream on top—is delicious, and makes me feel like Laura Ingalls Wilder on the prairie every time I eat it.

"Your mother is going to be very nervous today, kids," Dad counseled us as he sipped at his coffee. "This is a lifelong dream, so she's feeling a lot of pressure to succeed. She may or may not want our help; we just have to be ready but not get in the way. Okay?"

I nodded sleepily, and Tanner just sat there licking

his oatmeal spoon. "Any more?" he asked. I hadn't realized he had already finished. He lifted his bowl to lick around the inside of it, like a dog.

"Tanner! Seriously? What's happened to your table manners?" I reprimanded him.

But my dad headed off the bickering before it could begin. "No fighting today. Just let her know you're there for her. Okay?"

I nodded at him, chastened.

I was excited and nervous for Mom. I wanted the store to be a huge success, and I hoped tons of people would come. But I was also nervous for her. I hoped it wouldn't be so many people that she couldn't handle it or that she'd run out of ice cream or something. And I didn't want it to be embarrassing, like if no one came. I just wanted it to be good. We had called her the night before, and she'd sounded a little lonely, I thought. I'd asked if she wanted us to come home, and she'd said she had a ton of paperwork to do and that we should have fun with Dad. It was really hard needing to be in two places at the same time and thinking you weren't in the right one.

My dad took us to the new house at eight o'clock,

and we picked up a load of things that Mom needed at the store. She was already there, cleaning and putting the finishing touches on everything. It was weird for me to see my dad in our new house; he was already out of place. He kind of just stood in the hallway, not even plunking himself down onto a chair or anything like he normally would when we came home. I think he felt it too, because he kind of hustled to get out of there, like he was spying on her and didn't want to get caught. It made me sad.

At the store Tanner and I did little tasks, and my parents did big tasks, and pretty soon it was opening time. A reporter from the local paper was the first arrival, and she asked my mom a ton of questions and took some photos to run with the article. My mom gave her all sorts of samples, and she really loved everything. When the reporter left, we congratulated Mom but were shocked when she was upset.

"No one was here! I looked like a failure!" she wailed.

My dad laughed in surprise. "You've been open for only ten minutes. And it's still morning! I think it was great that she came when she did. You had time to answer all her questions and give her samples.

What if she came during a rush and you didn't have time to get your message out there?"

"What message?" asked Tanner.

I sighed in exasperation. "'Molly's Ice Cream is handmade with love. It's thick and creamy and good for the soul.' Where have you been?" Tanner shrugged and helped himself to a small cup of mini M&M's.

"Don't eat all my profits!" scolded my mom, flicking a dishtowel at him as he shoved them into his mouth. "Okay, quick. Here come some customers. Act natural!"

I picked up a broom and swept some imaginary crumbs up from the floor, while Tanner turned his back and neatened up the already-neat row of ice cream scoopers on the back counter. My dad ducked into the kitchen to do something there, and my mom helped her very first customers ever.

After they left, we hugged her, and that was basically the last time we had a chance to speak to her for the rest of the day.

Families poured in, one after another, all on their way to the beach for the day. At some point my dad ran out and got a pizza, and we each took a turn scarfing down slices back in the kitchen, out of view. The work was hard—physically demanding, and tiring because you had to be friendly and chatty with everyone—but I ended up being pretty good at it. Tanner lost interest quickly and got his friend Michael's mom to come pick him up. My dad had to run to the grocery store for more napkins, and there was a little bit of a lull around one o'clock, as people ate their lunches somewhere. My mom and I quickly wiped down tables, cleaned the countertops, swept straw wrappers from the floor, and grabbed more rolls of coins from the safe.

"Good job, Mama," I said as we raced past each other in our tasks.

"Thanks, sweetheart. You're an angel for helping me, and you're a natural at it."

"I think we've got this!" I said. But little did I know.

Right then, in walked Colin with a friend of his from school, and I was back on duty. We joked around while I gave them tons of samples and then made them each a sundae with my mom's trademark Kitchen Sink ice cream (crumbled pretzels and potato chips with fudge and caramel in a vanilla bean base). My mom was happy to see me with a friend from

Vista Green, and she smiled approvingly at Colin when I introduced them, which made me proud. I was really happy he had come. It made me feel like I had a real friend at my new school.

Right as Colin was leaving, in walked Tamiko and Sierra. I introduced them all in passing, and everyone was polite, but it wasn't like they had a chance to become great friends right in the doorway, so that was frustrating.

Tamiko and Sierra arrived at the counter super-excited and full of ideas, but my mom couldn't chat. If she wasn't helping a customer, she was refilling the paper goods or swapping out almost-empty tubs of ice cream. They wanted to talk to me, too, but my mom needed my help. I set them up on stools at the counter with an ice cream each (on the house, my mom insisted) and a pad of paper and pens and asked them to write down every idea they had, and anything they overheard people saying, good or bad. When it was quiet, we would chat a bit, but I had to stay behind the counter in case a customer came in. It was hard for me to watch Tamiko and Sierra out there, heads bent together; I wished I could join them. It was always the three of us before.

The best thing about the day was that people loved the ice cream, and I was super-proud. But I started to notice a funny thing: people didn't know what they wanted. Sometimes people would come up, all excited to try something new, but then they'd just chicken out and default back to basics and say, "Oh, you know what? I'll just have chocolate chip in a cone." It made me sad that people weren't willing to take a chance on something new and different—because, hey, you never know! Maybe the new thing would be even better than the old one. Or maybe you'd love them both! I promised myself I'd think about this later when I had some peace and quiet.

The traffic kept coming, which was good for business and bad for time with friends. Tamiko and Sierra were so close—right in front of me!—but I was scooping and sprinkling and had both hands busy as I tried to keep up with the orders. Suddenly Tamiko and Sierra spun around.

"Kenz!" cried Tamiko.

"Niña!"

There she was again—the girl from the mall. Tamiko and the other girl raced across the shop to hug each other. Thankfully, Sierra did not. Whether that was because she was eating ice cream or not wanting to hurt my feelings, I wasn't sure, but I appreciated it either way.

"Come meet Allie!" said Tamiko happily.

My palms were damp, and I gulped hard as they headed toward me. I plastered a fake-ish smile on my face (it was the best I could muster) and waited.

"Hi," said the girl. "I'm MacKenzie. I've heard so much about you. Your friends miss you so much. It's nice to finally meet you."

"Hi," I said. "I'm Allie."

We looked at each other for an awkward second. MacKenzie was very pretty, with beautiful pale skin and some freckles, like mine, sprinkled across her upturned nose. She had hazel eyes and dimples, and something about her smile just made her look like she was a nice person.

"Okay, you two weirdies," interrupted Tamiko. "New friend, old friend, no one's replacing anyone, no one needs to fill anyone's shoes. Let's just all be friends."

I burst out laughing, and so did MacKenzie. "Tamiko!" I cried.

"What? I broke the ice!" she said. "Or should I

say, ice *cream.*" Then she laughed at her own joke.

I shook my head. "You are too much."

Tamiko continued. "Oh, hey. I forgot to mention this to you, Allie. MacKenzie's a huge Anne what's-her-name fan, like you."

"Anne Shirley?" I said eagerly. "Anne of Green Gables?"

MacKenzie nodded vigorously and pointed to her bright red hair. "With hair like this, how could I not love her?" She grinned. "My mom loved the books so much growing up because she has red hair too. She prayed I'd be a redhead like Anne, and she even named me after her: MacKenzie Anne!"

"No way!" I said reverently. "You are so lucky! Which book in the series did you like reading the most?"

MacKenzie shook her head in embarrassment. "I'm a terrible reader. It's just really hard for me. Sierra keeps wanting me to work on Book Fest with her, but I just can't spare the time; I need it for my homework. My mom has actually read all the Anne books to me aloud, and I've seen all the movies."

I was really glad I wasn't being replaced by her at Book Fest. That would have been tough. "It's so nice to meet you," said MacKenzie. "Oh, and could I please have a peppermint shake?"

"Of course!" I said, and I happily set about making it. MacKenzie left after finishing her shake and said again it was nice to meet me. I said the same.

As the next hour or so wore on, people's beach days ended and we got slammed. Like, really slammed. At that point my mom and I got overwhelmed, and Tamiko and Sierra offered to help. They washed their hands and sanitized them, then threw on some starchy white aprons and jumped behind the counter to serve ice cream. It was sometime during this rush that Amanda and Eloise from Vista Green came in with Amanda's little sister. I was so happy they had accepted my invitation to come—it meant a ton to me—but I couldn't really talk. They got their order filled by my mom and then popped over to say hi to me after.

I quickly introduced them to Tamiko and Sierra, who were really sweet to them, and I felt a happy, warm feeling about where all my friendships were heading. Now all of my friends had met, and I had finally met MacKenzie.

At the end of the day my dad came back from running errands and insisted that my mom, my friends, and I take a break. Things had slowed down a lot, and though we anticipated an uptick again later, we gratefully accepted. My dad threw on an apron, and my mom and I made ourselves an ice cream, and we all sat down for a few minutes at the table.

"Great job, Mrs. S.!" said Tamiko.

My mom smiled a weary but pleased smile at us all. "It went pretty well, didn't it?"

"*Really* well," said Sierra.

"I guess I need to rethink my staffing requirements," said my mom, rubbing her forehead with the palm of her hand while she closed her eyes. "At least on weekends."

"Yeah," I agreed. "This is definitely not a one-lady job."

"Girls, I can't thank you enough for pitching in today like that," said my mom to my friends. "I'm going to pay you for your time." She stood and went to the cash drawer.

"No! Please, Mrs. S. It's on the house," joked Tamiko. "You don't need to pay us. Our parents would kill us if we took money from you on opening day."

My mom laughed. "Okay. Well, then free ice

cream for a week. How does that sound?"

"Be careful what you wish for," cautioned Tamiko, and we all laughed because we knew Tamiko could eat a week's worth of ice cream in a single day.

My mind was spinning. It was so fun hanging out with my besties like old times, and I couldn't bear how lonely it was without them. I thought back to my conversation with Sierra about needing a regular hangout time each week, and suddenly I had a great idea!

"Hey, Mom? What if the three of us worked for you, say, every Sunday?"

"*Ooh*, that would be awesome!" said Sierra.

Tamiko nodded. "Super-fun. As long as we could keep the baseball game on in the back so I could check it from time to time." Tamiko was a baseball nut; she and her grandfather in Japan video-chatted every week during baseball season to discuss their fantasy teams.

My mom stood still, thinking.

"Hmm, Mom? What do you say?" I asked.

"Well, every week is a big commitment. And you have homework and activities, and—"

"You don't have to pay me!" I said. "I'm your kid.

You could just pay them. It would be great!"

Mom laughed. "It's not just the money, Allie."

"Mama?" I said, looking into her eyes. "Please, Mama? I miss my friends. And this way I could still see them every week. Plus we would be *helping* you!"

My dad came out of the back room and exchanged glances with my mom. His eyebrows went up as if to say, *What's going on?* I looked at him pleadingly.

"It would be a great way to learn about a business, and we'd learn new responsibilities."

"Well," said Mom, "first we'd need to check with Tamiko's and Sierra's parents. Then we'd need to make sure that your homework is done and that working here every Sunday wouldn't get in the way of other commitments you all have."

"And that you can make the commitment weekly," said Dad, and Mom nodded.

"That's a lot of ifs," said Tamiko.

"Well, if we get past all those ifs," said my mom, "then we could do a trial run next Sunday. Ten dollars an hour each. If it works out, then you can do the Sunday shift."

The three of us squealed and hugged. "Awesome!" I cried. Then I ran and gave Mom a hug.

"I need to talk to your parents first, though."

Tamiko, Sierra, and I squeezed one another's hands. This could be great! We'd all be together every Sunday. We'd be having fun, plus we'd be making money, too! What could be better than that? Things were finally starting to look up for me. Suddenly life seemed as sweet as a chocolate cone again.

CHAPTER EIGHT
BOOK REVIEW

Colin was grinning as I joined him on the bus the next morning. I had to admit, I was pretty wiped out from being on my feet all day the day before. I couldn't believe my mom had to get up and do it all over again, but she was so excited that she didn't even mind.

Colin held up his hand for a high five, and I smacked it. "Awesome opening!" he crowed.

"Thanks," I said. "The whole day was a whirlwind."

"The store is going to be a huge success. I want to do an article about it in the school paper, with a photo of you at the store. I'm pitching the story at the editorial meeting today."

"Wow! Cool! Thank you!" I said, beaming. That

kind of publicity would sure help bring kids into the store.

"The flavors are awesome," said Colin. "I loved the Lemon Blueberry that I got, but there are so many more I'd like to try."

I smiled. "It's funny you should say that. I've noticed that certain kinds of people just get excited and go for it. They want to experiment and try everything. Other people get overwhelmed with the choices and end up kind of copping out and picking something really basic."

"They don't know what they're missing!" agreed Colin.

I decided to share an idea I'd had the night before while I'd been reading before I went to sleep. "I was thinking, it would be cool to have a little question ready for people, to help loosen them up when they're having trouble ordering. Like, 'Who's your favorite fictional character?' And then I could suggest something based on that!"

Colin laughed. "That's an icebreaker, for sure. So if I said 'Harry Potter,' you'd say?"

I scoffed. "Too easy! Butterscotch Chocolate Chunk, of course. Try someone harder." I laughed.

As Colin thought, suddenly the word "Molly's" caught my ear from somewhere in the bus. It was the Mean Team, seated a row ahead of us across the aisle. Colin and I exchanged a glance and listened in.

"It's the hot new thing," one of them was saying. "It's going to be the new hangout, for sure."

"Everyone's talking about it today, but *I've* known about it for a while. I didn't have time to get there yesterday, but I'm going as soon as possible. I want to get some pics on my feed."

"All you care about is social media, Blair! I just want to try the flavors. I looked at the menu online, and they look delicious."

"Well, I heard the founder is a rock-star chef from New York City."

"No, I heard she's from Paris," cut in Palmer.

I shook my head slightly and giggled as I looked at Colin. He just raised his eyebrows and shook his head.

At lunch I sat with Colin, Amanda, and Eloise, and they were all raving about the store. Colin said he'd gotten the green light to do the article and wanted to start right away, so I texted my mom to see if it was okay for me to be interviewed. She agreed, reminding me to make sure I emphasized that everyone was welcome, there was something for everyone, and that everything was made from handwritten family recipes—all-natural and no preservatives.

Colin asked me a lot of questions about the store; how my mom gets her ice cream flavor ideas (One time—for her Cereal Milk flavor—it was from me and Tanner drinking the milk from our fruit-flavored cereal. Another was from a dessert from France she read about where a chef paired strawberries with balsamic vinegar.); and what had inspired the store's design. I mentioned that my mom used to be a financial officer. Colin stopped me. "Really?" he asked.

"Yeah," I said. "At my dad's company. Then they decided to get divorced, and she wanted to try something she had always wanted to do."

"That's really cool," said Colin. "I mean, not the divorce part."

"No," I said. Things had been so busy, I hadn't thought too much about the divorce. We were all just kind of living life like it was the new normal, after all.

"Divorce is hard," said Colin, looking down. "My parents got divorced a long time ago, but it's still tricky."

"'Tricky' is a good word for it," I said. Suddenly

I wanted to ask Colin a lot of questions. "It just happened right before school started."

"Oh, wow, so that's why you're in a new school?" asked Colin. I nodded. "Well, let me know if you want to talk about it. Right now, though, I have to get this interview done."

"Shoot," I said.

He grinned. "Okay, so is the intent of your mom's place to give the kids a hangout after school? Is she trying to make it a social spot?" I thought about that for a second, especially after hearing the Mean Team talk about it.

"I think the intent is to sell really yummy ice cream," I said, thinking of my mom. "But it's definitely going to be the after-school social spot. And the best part is, *everyone* is invited." I thought of the Mean Team.

I guess it was unavoidable that I would have to deal with the mean girls at the shop sooner or later. That afternoon, after school, I walked straight to Molly's when I got off the bus. My mom was working—tired but happy—and there was a small but steady trickle of customers, just enough for one person to handle.

I checked in on my group chat with Tamiko and Sierra, as we had been doing every day after school at this time, but they didn't reply. I felt a little pang, but I didn't freak all the way out. I did some homework for a bit, but I was restless, so I made myself a small scoop of Banana Pudding ice cream in a cup and sat down to cast a critical eye around the shop. What did it look like to strangers? People who didn't know my mom or have the same taste as her? Was it welcoming? Appealing?

As I let the cool banana cream slide down my throat and I chewed on the salty-sweet Nilla wafers that were chunked through it, I decided the store was objectively beautiful and welcoming but maybe a little cold. It needed a tiny bit more personality to show through. I eyed an empty built-in bookshelf to the side of the window counter, and the wheels started spinning in my head.

"Hey, Mom?" I said during the next lull. "What if I brought in some books—some picture books, and kids' novels, and maybe a couple of books for grown-ups—and filled the bookshelf over there with them? People could borrow books or just look at them or read them while they're eating their ice cream."

My mom looked at the shelf with her head tipped to the side. "I had originally been thinking of doing jars of colorful lollipops there for display, but we could try books," she said. "Actually, I really love that idea, Allie. It would make the store more . . ."

"Homey!" I said, smiling.

"Yes!" she said.

I couldn't wait to curate the shelf with a selection of books I thought would appeal to customers—I might even try to look for books with ice cream themes. Maybe I'd even have a chance to make book recommendations as I served ice cream!

I was picking up my cup and used napkins when the bell above the door jingled. I turned, and there was the Mean Team.

My stomach dropped. On some level I'd known they were coming and that it would likely be soon, but it had seemed sort of unreal, like a distant possibility.

They looked at me and were also shocked, I think. Blair's eyes widened and then narrowed, seeing me in my apron, and Maria glanced at me and gave a half smile. Palmer kind of waved, but it was so fake, she could have been waving at her own reflection in the mirror behind me.

As they walked toward the freezer cases, the bell jingled again and lots of customers—little kids with parents, other middle school kids, a landscaping crew—all poured in at once.

"Allie! I need you!" called my mom.

"On it!" I said, and I turned my back to the Mean Team and went to wash up. I spun around to help the first customer, and it was Blair. Her eyes widened. "You *work* here?" she said.

"Yes," I said, smiling tightly. "Actually, my mother owns the store."

She raised her eyebrows and looked at the other mean girls. "Okay. I'll have a Lemon Blueberry scoop and a Balsamic Strawberry scoop in a cup. Not too big."

Please, I corrected her in my mind automatically, then turned to prepare her order. I could see in the mirror to my right that they were having a silent conversation with gestures and facial expressions, but when I turned to present the ice cream to Blair, they all acted natural.

She looked at the cup in her hand. "You didn't spit in it, did you?"

I was shocked. "What?!"

The other girls looked uncomfortable, but Blair looked at me again. "Did you *spit* in my *ice cream*?"

"Blair, come on," said Palmer. "She's just kidding," she said to me nervously.

I saw my mom glance over to see what was going on, but I didn't meet her eye. I stared levelly at Blair.

"I would never do anything to an ice cream except make it as delicious as humanly possible," I said in my calmest voice. "This is my family's store, and my great-grandmother's name is on the door. Anyway, who would spit in someone's ice cream?"

Maria tittered. "Blair would!"

I looked at Maria carefully. "Maybe you need a new friend, then."

Blair scoffed. "I was only kidding. And I wouldn't spit in someone's ice cream, anyway, Maria. Thanks a lot. How much do I owe you?" She smiled at me, but the smile didn't reach her eyes. I could tell she was embarrassed.

"It's on the house," I said, thinking of the phrase "kill them with kindness." It was one of my dad's favorites. "What can I get you two?" I turned my full attention to Maria and Palmer, as if Blair didn't exist.

"No, I'm happy to pay," Blair protested, but I

waved my hand without even looking at her.

"It's a write-off. A marketing expense." I'd heard my mom say that about free samples, and I felt super-sophisticated saying it, like a real businesswoman.

"Okay, thanks?" said Blair skeptically. I could tell she wondered why I would do something nice for her when she'd been so mean to me, but I had to think about what was good for Molly's.

Palmer was all charm now. "Could I please try the Banana Pudding in a sugar cone? It sounds delicious!"

"It's my favorite flavor of the day," I said, acting cheerful.

"Is there a tip jar?" asked Blair, waving a five-dollar bill at me.

All I needed was a tip from Blair. "No. But thanks anyway." We hadn't done that yet; my mom wasn't sure she liked the idea.

I presented Palmer with her order and asked Maria what she wanted. "I don't know. I can't decide. Maybe I'll just have vanilla."

As I'd been telling Colin, I really felt bad when people didn't go for something interesting at our store. It wasn't that our basic flavors weren't good; they were delicious. It was just that it usually seemed like a person picked them because the person was intimidated or uncreative, either of which could have been the case here. It was time to try my idea.

"Okay, wait. I'm going to help you pick a more interesting flavor by giving you our ice cream personality test. Who's your favorite character, from a book or movie?"

"What?" Maria was confused.

"Just work with me. Who?"

Blair and Palmer exchanged a giggle.

But Maria rose to the challenge. "Um, I guess Harriet the Spy?"

"Harriet? Seriously, Maria?" Blair laughed. Maria's face was red, but she stood her ground.

"Yes. It was my favorite book when I was little."

"And it's a great one," I agreed. "Okay, Harriet loved tomato sandwiches. We haven't made tomato ice cream yet, but another thing Harriet loved was cake and milk, every day after school, right?"

Maria's eyes lit up. "Yes! At three forty every day!"

"Yes. So why don't you channel Harriet and try our Devil's Food flavor? It's a plain cream base with chunks of double-chocolate cake in it—cake and milk, get it?"

"Okay!" said Maria. I could tell she was glad to be guided into a more interesting choice, and I was proud that my strategy had worked the first time, and on an enemy, no less!

"And I think you should drink it, in honor of Harriet. A Devil's Food milkshake, with one of our extra-wide straws, coming up."

"Perfect." Maria's eyes shone with satisfaction, and when I presented the shake to her and she sipped it, she closed her eyes and hummed with happiness. "This is so good!" she said.

"And so is Harriet the Spy," I said. "One of my faves."

Once they all had their ice cream, Blair turned to me.

"Bye, Allie," she said, and they all left.

"Bye. Thanks for coming in," I said with a wave. I turned to my next customer, my heart pounding in my chest.

I couldn't believe I'd just had the courage to stand up to a bully! Not only that, I'd definitely won that round. What's more, my new ice cream recommendation strategy had worked! And the funny thing was, the first person I wanted to tell about it was Colin.

That night my mom came into my room for a chat. She wanted to know what had happened with the girls at the store—she'd sensed something was amiss, but she'd been too busy to come over and check in. When I told her how I'd handled it, she scooped me up into a huge hug.

"Allie Shear, you're the best!"

"Mmmsh!" I said, my voice muffled in her shoulder. Maybe it was babyish to like a hug from your mom, but this one felt extra good.

She let me go and smiled at me, and her eyes were a bit moist. "Dad and I have really put you kids through a lot, and you've both handled it so well. I'm so proud of you."

"Thanks, Mama. I'm proud of you, too."

"And I just wanted to let you know, I've run the numbers, and I think it would be a great thing if you and Tamiko and Sierra came to work with me at the shop."

"Mom!" I dive-bombed her with another hug.

"Okay, but hang on," she said, holding me off at arm's length. "I need to discuss this with Tamiko's and Sierra's parents. It's on a trial basis. I need to see that you girls are taking it seriously, and I will pay you. If it works, you can come every Sunday. That way you can help me out and learn some responsibility in a job, but you can also see your friends."

"Thank you, Mom. We're going to do a great job! And look—" I gestured to the milk crate of books I'd pulled from our collection to put on the shelf at the store. "Those are for our customers. Maybe you can bring them tomorrow in your car, and I'll arrange them when I get there after school."

She ruffled my hair. "Perfect. Thanks, sweetheart. Love you."

"Love you too, Mama."

As soon as she left the room, I lunged off my bed for my phone and texted Tamiko and Sierra. I still hadn't heard from them since our after-school check-in time. Where were they?

CHAPTER NINE

A TASTE OF RESPONSIBILITY

When I woke up the next morning and still hadn't heard from Tamiko and Sierra, I was upset. I turned my phone on and off. Still nothing. I didn't want to get crazy, but I started to feel forgotten. As I waited for the bus, I called Tamiko's phone, and she finally picked up.

"Ali-baba!" she cried.

"Where have you guys been?" I asked.

"Oh, Sierra totally dropped the ball on the Book Fest plans, unsurprisingly, so she roped me and MacKenzie into bailing her out. We were at MacKenzie's until so late last night, I barely had time to get my homework done. I'm sorry I didn't reply yet about the store. That's great news. We do have a Book Fest meeting on

Sunday, but it should be fine. I don't think it will run too long."

I stared at the phone in my hand, unable to comprehend what was happening, on so many levels. Sierra had gotten Tamiko to work on the Book Fest? I'd tried for two years to get her involved, and she wouldn't budge, saying she didn't like books and wanted to save the trees they were printed on. And why had they all been at MacKenzie's? Shouldn't they have worked on it at school, with Mrs. Olson?

My stomach churned and my jaw clenched as the bus rolled up. I didn't even know what to say to Tamiko, so instead I just said, "What? I can't hear you! Bad connection," and hung up, my hands shaking.

I trudged up the bus steps, and as soon as I hit the aisle, I heard someone calling my name.

"Allie! Over here!"

"Allie!"

It was the Mean Team, waving me over to join them.

Just behind them, across the aisle, was Colin, smiling and waving.

As I drew near the mean girls, Blair patted the seat next to her, smiling. "Come. Right here."

Still angry from my phone call with Tamiko, I was

in no mood to play nice. I smiled a tight smile and shook my head. "I'm sitting with my friend Colin over there. He's right past *the pool*," I said, and kept walking. I wondered if they remembered the pool prank they'd played on me the first day.

The girls were silent as I joined Colin. They remembered.

"Hey," I said, settling in.

"Hey," he said. "I don't mind if you sit with them."

I sighed. "Thanks. I'd rather start my day off with someone nice."

He rolled his eyes. "Yeah. But it might not be a bad strategy to sit with them sometimes, you know? Like, keep your friends close but keep your enemies closer?"

We laughed. "Thanks," I said. "But not today, that's for sure. Today I kind of just want things to be normal, not different."

I was really upset about Tamiko and MacKenzie and Book Fest, but before I knew it, it was almost Sunday again and time to have my first official afternoon as an employee of Molly's, with Tamiko and Sierra. On Saturday night, we had a check-in by phone.

"The Book Fest committee meeting is at eleven

thirty tomorrow," said Tamiko. "If we're not finished in time for us to get to work at one, we'll just leave early."

"Yup," agreed Sierra.

"Okay, guys. Just remember, this is our test. We've got to do a good job or my mom won't take us seriously." I really did not want to mess this up, for our sakes and my mom's.

Sierra nodded on my tiny phone screen, with big, earnest eyes. "Yes, Allie. I'll make it! I'm saving up to learn mountain climbing. I said I'd join the mountaineering club at school, so I need all the gear—and I really need the money."

Tamiko and I sighed in exasperation, and Tamiko said, "Well, I need it for my toilet customization fund."

"Tamiko!" I laughed. "I was joking, remember?"

"One person's joke is another person's treasure!" said Tamiko.

"Okay, wait. Before you hang up, Allie," said Sierra. "Um, how many volunteers do you think we need for Book Fest?"

"Well, how many do you have?" I asked.

There was a brief silence. "Um, three? Me, Tamiko, and MacKenzie?"

My eyes nearly popped out of my head. "Sierra!

You'll need at least ten kids to lug in the boxes and set up the books on all the tables. Then a rotating schedule of two per shopping session—they can miss sports for it but no academic classes. Then you need at least fifteen kids to clean up: to repack the boxes, throw away the empties, break down displays, whatever. I guess it could be the same fifteen to twenty kids, but . . ." I paused. "Have you made an announcement in assembly?"

"Oh, Allie," wailed Sierra. "I wish you were here to do it. You're so good at all this. Oh, why did I ever say yes?"

Tamiko and I glanced at each other as Sierra buried her head in her hands. This was how it always went: Sierra would overcommit, and Tamiko and I would bail her out, with mixed results.

I began to walk them through what they needed to do, and I forced Sierra to take good notes on what I said. For goodness' sake, I didn't even go to their school anymore and I felt like I was still running Book Fest. The funny thing was, I didn't miss it as much as I'd thought I would.

On Sunday, Dad dropped me off at Molly's at twelve thirty. He reminded me that I needed to treat this as a real job, not just as catch-up time with my friends, and that Mom was really counting on us. "Promise, Allie?" he said.

"Scoop's honor," I said, holding my hand to my heart, and he laughed.

"Mom told me about what happened with the girls from the new neighborhood," said Dad. I was surprised. I mean, I knew Mom and Dad still talked, but I didn't know how that was going to work. I guess they had to talk about me and Tanner.

"I know it's hard," Dad said, "but—"

"I know, I know," I said. "Better. Better. Better." I sighed.

"Well, yes," said Dad, "but I was going to say that it's going to take some time. And that even if I don't live in the house with you all the time, I'm still here if you need me."

I realized that I hadn't actually seen Dad too much this past week. It had gone by so fast. I thought about him in his apartment by himself and wondered if he was lonely without us.

"Now," he said, hitting the auto-unlock in the car, "go forth and scoop."

"Will do!" I said.

"And if you encounter a bully," he said, turning serious, "then just—"

I waited.

"Cone them with kindness."

"Dad!" I sputtered, and giggled. He grinned. I scrambled out of the car.

I waved to Mom, who was with a customer, and headed to the back of the store. I tied a crisp white apron at my waist and washed up.

We were at the lunchtime lull, as my mom had come to call it. Noon to one thirty was a great time for her to return calls and get some business stuff done, since it was always quiet while people were off having their lunches. Then we'd get hit hard for an hour from one thirty to two thirty. After that, business would slow to a trickle, and then we'd get really socked at four o'clock as people left the beach or came home from soccer games or whatever. By five thirty things were usually quiet again, though there was an after-dinner rush on Fridays and Saturdays.

I checked my watch as a customer with two kids walked in. It was twelve fifty-three, and there was still no sign of Tamiko and Sierra. I was stressed and annoyed. Were they going to let me down?

I finished up with the lady and her two kids, and while they sat to eat, I peeked at my phone, which I'd tucked into my back pocket. As luck would have it, my mom walked in from her back office right then.

"Allie! Remember what I said! No phones on duty!"

"Sorry! I just was checking this once . . ." I didn't want to finish my sentence and highlight the fact that Tamiko and Sierra were late. But luckily I didn't have to! Tamiko came bounding into the store in a T-shirt she'd made—it had pictures of sprinkles and ice cream cones all over it, and it said *Molly's* in flowing script across the back, in the same exact font as my mom's store window.

Luckily, the awesomeness of the T-shirt distracted my mom from the fact that it was now exactly twelve fifty-nine. While Tamiko washed and aproned up, I turned to help another customer. By the time Tamiko was at my side and my mom had gone back to the kitchen, I was able to huff, *"Where is Sierra?"*

Tamiko rolled her eyes. "She'll be here shortly. I finally insisted I had to leave, and I said she should do the same, but she had 'just one more thing' to do."

"Annoying," I said. "I knew that was going to happen."

Tamiko laughed. "Didn't we all! I promise, Allie, I'll be here early from now on."

I squeezed Tamiko in a sideways hug. "Thanks, *chica*. Or *niña*. Whatever you go by these days."

"I like to go by 'Allie Shear's best friend,'" Tamiko said.

It made me feel better to hear that.

It wasn't until one twenty-five that the jingling of the door caused me to look up from the banana split I was making. In walked Sierra, red-faced and huffing. She raced into the back to ditch her stuff, then raced behind the counter, strapping on her apron as she came.

"Wash your hands!" hissed Tamiko. I was glad she'd said it and not me.

In a panic, Sierra knocked over a metal milkshake canister that was mostly empty but dirty, so it splattered chocolaty milk all over. Mom was working the cash register and glanced over. As Sierra bent to clean it up, I could see she was crying.

I squatted down next to her so that the customers couldn't see me. "Sierra. I'll clean it up. Go take a minute in the bathroom to calm down, okay?"

She nodded and fled while I heaved a heavy sigh. Soon the customers had all been helped, Tamiko and I had cleaned everything up, and Sierra emerged, calmer and clear-eyed. She came behind the counter and washed up again.

I wanted to be mad at her—mostly because this happened all the time—but now that I wasn't with her all the time, I could see that things were a legitimate challenge for her in a way they weren't for me and Tamiko. Time management, planning, organization of materials—Sierra couldn't do it alone.

We couldn't really have a conversation while we worked, so we didn't address anything about Book Fest or Sierra's shortcomings as an employee. But we did end up having fun.

Tamiko's sassy personality was great with customers. If they ordered something that she thought was too plain or boring, she'd push them to be more adventurous, always making them laugh in the process. Like when a bald, middle-aged dad came in and copped out by ordering a vanilla shake, Tamiko leaned over the counter and said, "Dude. What would your seventeen-year-old self say to you now if he saw you ordering a vanilla shake? Come on. You owe it to yourself to have a little more fun than that. I bet you had a wild youth!" The guy roared with laughter, and he changed his order to a triple banana split! If I had one complaint about Tamiko, it might be that she spent *too* much time with each customer. The line grew pretty long at one point, and I had to nudge her to move her along.

Where Tamiko was jazzy, Sierra was sweet. She was good with the little kids who dropped their ice cream, soothing their tears as she replaced their cones. She was great with grandmas who wanted to chat a lot about the weather. If she had one flaw, it was probably that she made the scoops too big; she was too generous with the product. But I didn't want to be harsh on her on her first real day, especially not with the beginning she'd had. Plus, Mom was really the boss, not me. And so far at least, Mom seemed pretty pleased. She kept looking over and smiling at us. Maybe because I was smiling a lot too.

My best idea of the day was that I put a tiny pinch of sprinkles on top of each ice cream when I made it. It started by accident, when I thought someone wanted sprinkles, but they stopped me, so only about twelve sprinkles landed on top of their ice cream. The customer laughed it off and called it "a little sprinkle of happy."

For the rest of the day, the girls and I would put tiny smatterings of sprinkles on each ice cream and say, "Here's a sprinkle of happy!" and people loved it.

As our shift drew to a close, there was a bit of a lull. We helped my mom load her ice cream into the deep freeze in the back of the store.

"Good start today, girls. I appreciate your being on time and working so hard."

The three of us exchanged uneasy glances. Had she not noticed that Sierra had been almost half an hour late?

"Next week I'll probably assign you some tasks that you can rotate through. Two people on the counter and one doing other stuff, like cleaning the fridge or smashing cookies for toppings."

We all agreed, and then Tamiko spoke up. "Mrs. S., I had a few ideas for some ice cream designs. Would you let me try some next time if I sent you some photos to show what we could do?"

"Sure, Tamiko. Thanks. If we can do them economically and it doesn't take too long or make too much of a mess, I'd always be up for trying cool new things."

"Great! Because I have tons of ideas for rainbow-dipped cones, and unicorn sundaes, and mermaid pops—"

"Okay, okay, I get it!" said my mom, putting her palms in the air in surrender.

We all laughed. Tamiko was never short on ideas.

"All right. Then let's say I'll see you three back here next Sunday at twelve forty-five. That way you're all set and ready for a one o'clock start. If tardiness stays an issue, this won't work."

I cringed. I guessed she *had* noticed Sierra's late arrival. Sierra blushed and nodded, but Tamiko lightened the mood by saying, "We love our sprinkle Sundays, don't we, girls? Hey, get it? Sprinkle *sundaes*?" We all laughed. "We're the Sprinkle Sunday sisters!" Tamiko added, and we all dove in for a group hug, including Mom.

We hung up our aprons and helped ourselves to an ice cream each while we waited for Mrs. Sato. I showed Tamiko and Sierra the book corner Mom and I had arranged. So far it seemed like a good idea. Right then one woman was reading *Olivia* to two kids as they ate their ice cream. And earlier in the day I'd seen a little girl pick up a copy of *Anne of Green Gables* and not want to put it down when they left, which had made me really happy.

"Oh, I remember this book!" said Sierra, picking up a picture book. "I used to love this one."

Just then the bell over the door jingled, and we all looked up. In walked the Mean Team, and my heart dropped as they sauntered over to our table.

Blair cast an appraising eye over the group of us and sighed, shaking her head. "Still reading little kids' books, Allie?" she said, and snickered.

Tamiko bristled, but I put a hand on her leg to shush her.

"These are my friends, Blair. Why do you want to come in here and be mean to us?"

"It's a free country," said Blair with a shrug. Suddenly my mom came out from behind the counter and was standing by our side. "Hi, girls. What's going on? Can I help you with anything?"

I kept my eyes locked on Blair. "Nothing. Blair was just about to apologize, and then she was going to leave. Palmer and Maria want ice cream."

"Okay," said my mom, gathering Palmer and

Maria, one under each arm. "Let's get you girls something."

Alone, Blair's courage faltered; you could just see it evaporate. She looked at Palmer and Maria, who were both engrossed in choosing a flavor.

"It's not so easy being alone, is it, Blair?" I said quietly. "Imagine being the new girl at school and being alone. We don't have to be friends. But you can't come in here and insult me. I think you should leave now." Blair held my gaze for a few seconds, and then she turned to her friends.

"Palmer? Maria?" she said, but they ignored her.

She stood awkwardly for a minute in the middle of the store, and then she turned on her heel and left. As the door whooshed closed behind her, my friends cheered.

I was shaking, but I felt good. Sierra hugged me, and Tamiko patted my back.

Palmer and Maria had just paid, and they came back over to our table. Mom was hanging back, but close enough to hear.

"Sorry about Blair," said Palmer. "She's going through a bad stage, since her parents are getting divorced. Things are rough for her right now."

"There's no excuse for being mean," I said. "My parents are getting a divorce. It's hard, and sometimes it seems unfair, but it doesn't mean you can treat other people badly. Nothing gives you that excuse."

Maria leaned in to see the book. "Oh, I loved that one," she said, sighing. "I used to read it all the time."

"Me too," said Sierra.

"I think I still have my copy," said Maria.

"Oh, you totally do," said Palmer. She turned to us. "Maria has all of her books organized in her room just so. She never gets rid of any of them."

I tilted my head and looked at Maria, seeing her a little differently.

"Well, they're like old friends," she said, grinning. "And we don't get rid of old friends, do we?"

"We sure don't," said Sierra, giving me a squeeze.

"Well, thanks for the ice cream," said Palmer.

"See you at school, Allie," said Maria. And they left.

Sierra burst out, "Oh, Allie, you're just like Anne Shirley!"

I laughed a little. "Not really, but thanks for the compliment."

CHAPTER TEN

BOOK FEST

I avoided the Mean Team all the next day, even when Palmer and Maria shot me friendly and apologetic looks as I walked quickly past them on the bus. I sat with Colin at lunch, then raced to the library to help Mrs. K. start pulling books that hadn't been checked out in at least five years.

After school Sierra's mom picked me up, with Sierra and Tamiko in the car. It was just like old times! I had offered to help Sierra get organized for Book Fest, and she had gratefully accepted.

"Allie, Sierra told me how you had a showdown with the mean girls at the ice cream parlor. I'm so proud of you!" said Dr. Perez in the car.

"Thanks," I told her. "One of the hard things

about owning a store is that you have to let in any-one. It's not like you're inviting friends over to your house or something. It's open to the general public all the time."

"Yeah, even when the general public are jerks!" said Tamiko.

"You're right," Dr. Perez agreed. "But it's all about how you treat them and react to them. And you reacted beautifully."

Sierra's twin sister, Isabel, was home already, playing a video game.

"Hey, Isa!" I said, crossing the living room to give her a hug.

Isa was nice, but she'd gone in a totally different direction from Sierra. She was very focused and ath-letic; she was so good at soccer that she played on an all-boys high school travel team, the only girl. We used to be closer when we were little but had kind of drifted apart in recent years. We caught up for a few minutes, and I asked if she could volunteer to help with Book Fest. She said, "Sure!" It was a little odd that Sierra hadn't even asked her, but things were sometimes weird between them.

Up in Sierra's room I got out some graph paper and began making a few checklists. One was a timeline of what had to happen over the next few days, since Book Fest started Friday and ran through early next week. Another was a timeline for setup day, and another for breakdown day.

I had Sierra make a list of people she had asked to volunteer, and it was woefully short, so I had Ms. Social Media, Tamiko Sato, begin a campaign to recruit people on SuperSnap and anywhere else she could think of. Within half an hour we had ten kids; within an hour we had twenty.

"Wow! You make this look so easy, Allie!" said Sierra admiringly.

"It doesn't take a lot of time to get organized," I said. "You just need to know what you need. And I've done it before many times, so I have an idea."

I made a checklist of supplies (box cutters, large contractor garbage bags, a couple of cases of water for the volunteers, pens, and more).

After an hour and a half, Sierra was visibly more confident. The systems were all in place, Tamiko had assigned all the volunteers their time slots, and my work was done. But it was bittersweet leaving them when my dad pulled up at six. I didn't want to go.

Sierra could tell that I was a little down as I left. "We miss you, Allie. At least we still have Sprinkle Sundays, right?"

"As long as you're on time this Sunday, we will!" I joked.

Tamiko gave me a squeeze before I got into the car. It was unlike her to hug me, so I laughed and said, "What's the occasion?"

"You're a good friend," she whispered. "My hugs are like unicorns: they appear rarely and under very special circumstances. I know it's hard for you to work on this and not be able to go, and I'm sorry."

I took a deep breath. "It's okay. Really. I think it was maybe the planning and hanging out with friends part I missed the most."

Tamiko gave me another squeeze, and I left.

That night I cried a little in my bed as I was falling asleep. I tried to think of Anne Shirley for inspiration, but honestly, sometimes Anne Shirley just needed a good cry too. I fell asleep dreaming of unicorns and friends and ice cream and better things.

When the bell for gym class rang on Friday, I stood up from my desk in English and stretched. It would feel good to run around for a little while.

As I gathered my things, Colin sidled up to me. "Hey, Allie, I was wondering if you might want to do some book reviews for the paper? And maybe you could do an ice cream pairing with each one at the end."

I was so pleased! "Sure, Colin. Thanks! That would be really fun! What a cool idea."

He smiled and shook his head. "It was actually Maria's idea, if you can believe it. She explained in our editorial meeting how you'd done it for her, and we all thought it sounded really good. She even suggested a name for the column, Get the Scoop. Pretty cool, right?"

"Wow. Wonders never cease," I said. How interesting!

"Yeah," he said. "You know she really loves books too, right? She reads all the time. Anyway, I'll see you Sunday at Molly's!" He waved and left for his next class. Colin was coming to take a picture of me at the store to go with the article he'd written. "See you Sunday" had a nice ring to it. Maybe Molly's would be the next great hangout, for all my friends, old and new.

I felt a warm glow as I left Ms. Healy's room. When I stepped into the hall, there stood Mrs. K., dressed in a black sheath dress, with big fake pearl earrings, and her hair up in a bun. Her arms were crossed, and she appeared to have car keys in her hand, which she jangled at me.

"Okay, let's go. Got the permission. You need to stop by the office to sign out. Gather your things," she said, and she began walking toward the office.

"Um? What?" I scurried after her as she climbed the stairs. "Where are we going? I have everything I need." I always packed up before English because I liked to leave school straight from gym.

She didn't even turn around. "Book Fest. Let's go. I need to see it. Mrs. Olson invited me."

I stopped, stock-still, on the stairs. "Wait, *what*? You know Mrs. Olson?"

Mrs. K. kept walking, rounding the stairs and heading into the hallway, so I chased after her. "Come along. She and I were roommates in graduate school when we got our library degrees. I guess you could say she's my best friend."

Whaaaat? "Oh my gosh, so that's how you knew who I was when I came?"

"Yes. Mmm-hmm. She told me her favorite student was coming here."

"Why didn't you tell me?" We'd reached the office, and I quickly signed out. I noticed that Mom had already signed the permission form.

"Oh, didn't I tell you? I thought I had. Let's go. This way."

The trip to my old school was brief, and Mrs. K. and I chatted the whole way. It turned out she was also friends with Mrs. O'Brien at the bookstore. By the time we reached my old middle school, it had sunk in that I was actually going to Book Fest! I couldn't wait to surprise my friends.

In the lunchroom I ran into tons of kids and teachers who were happy to see me. Mrs. Olson gave me a huge hug and kept saying how much she missed me and how she appreciated my helping with Book Fest even though I'd left the school. I felt like a returning celebrity. Tamiko and Sierra screamed when they saw me, and we did a three-way dance, until I noticed MacKenzie standing to the side, and I thought, *Why not?* and grabbed her into our group to dance with us.

They had to hustle because the sixth grade was coming in for their shopping session shortly, and the author Maya Burns was arriving any minute, so they left me to browse or help as I wished. The only bummer was that I barely had any money. If I'd known I was coming, I would have brought my ice cream money from Sunday and my paltry savings.

When I looked up from the newest Cupcake Diaries book, my eyes went wide.

Maya Burns was crossing the room quickly with a huge smile on her face and a Molly's milkshake cup in her hand!

"Look!" said Sierra, spotting it at the same time as I did. We laughed like crazy.

"No way!" I said.

Just then a hand on my back pushed me into the line to get books signed. I looked up. Mrs. K. was handing me two copies of Maya Burns's book to get signed. "But I didn't bring any money," I said.

"Mmph, you bought this already," said Mrs. K.

"What?" I looked up, confused.

Mrs. K. smiled. "One for you and one for the library. You get both of these signed for me, okay?" Then she walked over to talk to Maya Burns.

Sierra stepped in line in back of me and said, "Oh, darn. Did you already buy her book? Because I bought you a copy this morning. I was going to get it signed by her and give it to you to say thanks for helping me with Book Fest." She handed me a copy of the paperback Mrs. K. had just given me.

"Oh no, me too!" said Tamiko, slipping a copy to me. "But mine's just because we miss you!"

We all laughed, and I thanked them gratefully. "This might be the best day of my life," I said.

"We know that, silly. You always love Book Fest," said Tamiko, whacking me on the shoulder (which was much more Tamiko's style than a hug).

Sierra sighed and shook her head regretfully. "I love it, but there is no way I'm running it next year," she said.

And then it was our turn at the table. As soon as we reached Maya Burns, Tamiko blurted, "That's her family's ice cream parlor! And we all work there on Sundays!" She gestured to the Molly's milkshake.

"Sprinkle Sundays!" I cried, and we all high-fived.

Ms. Burns was super-nice and friendly, and we chatted quickly as she signed the book for the library, then the copy Sierra had given me, which I was going to take to the store, and then the copy Tamiko had bought me, which I was going to take home to read. That left one copy. Maya Burns looked at me. "Should I make this out to someone special?"

I hesitated.

She tilted her head. "What's your favorite book?" she asked.

"*Anne of Green Gables!*" I said quickly.

"Oh, that's one of my favorites too!" she said. Then she scribbled "To a Kindred Spirit" in the front and signed her name. She winked as she handed it to me. "You never know when you'll find a kindred spirit to give this to," she said. "Sometimes they aren't that far away."

A kindred spirit. . . . Who knew there would be so many of them for me to find? Sure, I had my family and Tamiko and Sierra and Mrs. Olson. Now I also had Mrs. K., Ms. Healy, and even Colin maybe. But someone who loved books as much as I did . . . someone who loved Anne. Suddenly I knew—this book had to be for MacKenzie. You just never knew when you'd find a kindred spirit.

As Sierra, Tamiko, and I were saying our good-byes, Mrs. Olson and Mrs. K. darted to the table to say hi. I could hear Mrs. K. asking Ms. Burns to come to Vista Green for a visit, and Ms. Burns saying, "Sure, that would be lovely."

My friends and I chatted for a little bit longer, and then my mom texted to say she was outside to pick me up. We were going out for a casual family dinner with my dad, and I was looking forward to it.

"Get psyched for Sunday, Sprinkle Sisters!" said Tamiko.

"Sprinkle Sundays with my sisters," cheered Sierra.

"See you Sunday!" I called out. See you Sunday. Sundays with my Sprinkle Sisters. It had a really nice ring to it.

"Maybe we could do something like this at Vista Green," Mrs. K. said to me, "but maybe a little different. Maybe a little better."

"I'm all for that," I said. "A little different, but better." I hugged the book to my chest. A new book from one of my favorite authors! I couldn't wait to read it.

I thought about all the recent changes in my life. It was almost as if I were a character in a book. Maybe not Anne Shirley or Hermione Granger, but still interesting and exciting. What would the next chapter be in the life of Allie Shear? I couldn't wait to find out.

DON'T MISS BOOK 2:

CRACKS IN THE CONE

My best friend Allie squeezed my hand. "Happy Sprinkle Sunday," she whispered to me. Then she whispered the same thing into our other best friend Sierra's ear. I could sense both the nervousness and the excitement in Allie's voice. *Sprinkle Sunday*, I repeated in my head. It was finally here. And I did mean finally. I felt like we'd been waiting *forever*—even though it had only been a week since the last time we had all been here.

Allie's mom, Mrs. Shear (or, as I called her, Mrs. S.), had opened an ice cream shop after she'd divorced Allie's dad, and Mrs. S., Allie, and Allie's little brother had moved to another town. It was a whole lot of change, especially for Allie. But we were all really happy when Mrs. S. offered the three of us (that's me, Sierra, and

Allie) jobs at the ice cream store every Sunday. That was why we called ourselves the Sprinkle Sundays sisters.

Aside from our making some extra moolah (which my mom said should go toward a college fund, but I had other ideas) with the new gig, Mrs. S. had given us all cute T-shirts to wear with the shop name, Molly's Ice Cream. (Molly had been Allie's great-grandma, and she'd taught Mrs. S. how to make ice cream and had inspired the shop.) Plus, I got to spend some quality time with my two besties. I'd been super-excited about it all week. Until . . . well, until Sunday morning happened.

I was almost late for work, which would have been bad, because the previous week at our trial session Sierra had been super-late, and Mrs. S. had made it clear that it shouldn't happen again. But I slept through my alarm because I'd stayed up customizing my toilet seat with plastic fish and mermaid charms. It looked really cute, and it was going to make for a funny surprise for my guests. (Don't judge—it was Allie's idea, and it came out awesome.)

Anyway, I woke up to find Mom shaking me.

"Tamiko! You have to get ready," she said.

I groaned and pulled the pillow over my face. "I

think there are laws against waking up children by shaking them. It's cruel and unusual," I said.

Mom made a grunty sound. "Well, being late to work on your first day is cruel and unusual. Please get up—and pull your hair back off your face. You don't want to get hair in anybody's ice cream. That would *also* be cruel and unusual."

"I'm up, I'm up," I said. After my shower I quickly made two long braids in my hair and then pulled them back with a ponytail holder. Mom's advice was usually annoying, but she was right about the hair. Nobody wants an ice cream sundae with rainbow sprinkles and Tamiko DNA. Yuck! With a little extra hustle I was able to arrive right on time for our first shift.

After we all hugged hello, we heard a shuffle near the back door. It was Mrs. S., walking in with a tub of ice cream almost bigger than she was.

"Can you girls please help me bring in the ice cream from the van out back?" she asked. "We sold out of seven flavors yesterday!"

The three of us looked at one another. I guess it was time to, you know, work.

"I should have refilled the flavors last night, but I was just too tired," Mrs. S. continued, and then she turned to Allie. "Your dad was nice enough to bring them over to me today."

Right, Allie's dad. The weird thing about Allie's parents was that they always used to fight when they were married. Not like huge blowout fights but lots of little fights, which made us all squirm. They bickered in front of Allie and her little brother, Tanner, and even in front of Sierra and me. I'm pretty sure you're not supposed to fight in front of your daughter's friends, but we *did* go over to their house a lot, I guess. Nobody was really surprised when they got divorced, except for Allie. It's always different when it's your parents. But now that they were divorced, it was like they were best friends or something. They were super-smiley and helpful to each other. They probably got along better than my own parents, even.

We followed Allie's mom through the back door to the minivan that she used to haul stuff back and forth to the shop. She rented a space in an industrial kitchen somewhere else in Bayville, where she made the ice cream and stored it in a big Deepfreeze. Allie's dad was there now too, unloading the tubs, and Tanner was helping him—or doing Tanner's version of helping, which is to say, he watched us doing everything and complained that it was too hot outside.

"Hey, Mr. S.!" I said. "Hi, Tanner."

Before I could get another word in, Allie's mom took one of the tubs from Mr. S. "Enough talking!" she said. "We don't want the ice cream to melt."

"You heard the boss!" Mr. S. said, and we all laughed. Allie and Sierra grabbed buckets, and we lugged them through the back office and into the front parlor. I dumped the bucket into the bin marked VANILLA in one of the shop's long freezers. A curved glass top was open in the back so that we could scoop, but the glass protected the ice cream in the front from sneezing customers and little kids with icky hands. Besides vanilla, chocolate, and strawberry, Mrs. S. had concocted some truly special and delicious flavors, like Lemon Blueberry, Banana Pudding, Butterscotch Chocolate Chunk, and Maple Bacon.

"There's so much more vanilla than anything else," I said, looking at all the flavors lined up.

"It's Mom's best-selling flavor," Allie said.

"Really? Why would anyone get vanilla when there are so many cool things to try?" I asked.

"You know, I think part of the reason is that even the basic flavors are amazing," Allie said. "Mom's vanilla is the best vanilla around."

"It is definitely the most vanilla-y," Sierra chimed in. "I love it!"

"Vanilla-y! Is that even a word?" I teased.

"But also I think people just order the same thing out of habit," Allie went on.

"Well, they can eat as much vanilla as they like, as far as I'm concerned," Mrs. S. said, entering the parlor with a tub of ice cream. "They're still giving me business."

"I guess," I said. "But I love all of the exciting flavors. Do you have any new ones coming out soon?"

"I'm trying a new recipe with lavender, but I'm not sure what other flavors to pair with it," she replied. "I don't want it to be too flowery."

"Ooh, will it be purple? That is an awesome color for ice cream," I said, thinking about all of the cool stories people would post with purple ice cream in the frames.

She smiled. "I could definitely make it purple. Hmm. Maybe Lavender Blackberry?"

Then she turned to Allie. "I've got a bunch of ordering and bookkeeping to catch up on, so I'm going to leave you girls out front. You're in charge, Allie. You know what to do to set up. The afternoon rush will start soon!"

Allie nodded. "We got this!"

Mrs. S. disappeared into the back, and Allie faced us. She had a serious look on her face.

"Okay, here's the plan," she said. "Sierra, you're on the cash register because you're the best with numbers out of all of us."

Sierra gave a goofy salute. "I will make the mathletes proud!" she said.

"Tamiko, since you're such a great people person, you can take the orders," Allie went on. "I'll fill them, and then you can hand them to the customer."

"People person?" I asked. "You mean like a game show host? I can do that." I held up a scooper like a microphone. *All right, customer seventy-seven, it's time to play Hoop the Scoop!* I announced, and then pretended to bounce an invisible basketball around on the counter.

"Tamiko! Watch out!" Sierra scolded.

I looked over. The jar with candy buttons was wobbling. I'd almost knocked into it.

"A shaky landing for star people person Tamiko Sato," I hissed in a sports announcer voice, but Allie just sighed.

"Watch out, Ms. People Person," Allie said. "Or else you'll be the one cleaning the entire shop tonight."

"You wouldn't," I said menacingly.

"I so would," Allie said, but this time she was laughing.

Then the three of us cracked up. We actually did have to clean the store—wiping down the counters and tables, sweeping up, and washing out all the scoops—but Mrs. S. had a service come in and do the hard scrubbing, thank goodness.

"All right," Allie said once we caught our breath. "Can you guys help me get more spoons out of the storage room? And napkins. We need to refill the napkin dispensers too. And make sure all the ice cream cups are stacked up and ready."

After refilling one set of supplies, I took my phone out of my pocket.

"I'm going to take some photos and post them," I said. "You know, just to remind people that Sunday is a great day to come out for ice cream."

I dimmed the lights just a *little* to take the perfect snap.

"Okay. Sierra and I can handle the rest of the stuff, I guess," Allie said, but the way she said it, there was an edge in her voice.

Hmm. That was weird. Allie rarely had an attitude. The only time I'd really seen her get mad was when her parents got divorced and told her that she'd be moving and starting school in a new town. And to be honest that was totally understandable, because I'd be really mad about that too. But why was she annoyed now?

I wondered if I should tell her that good marketing is important for any business. I knew that because my brother, Kai, took marketing classes at the high school, and sometimes I helped him study by holding up his flash cards while I painted my nails.

Then I reminded myself that Allie probably wasn't actually mad. Maybe she was just trying to manage Sierra and get everything perfect for our first official day at work. Sierra was my other best friend, but she got distracted a lot and wasn't the most detail-oriented person. Plus she always took on too many things at once. We tried to help her, but sometimes things were a mess. I think Allie and I were both a little nervous about her dropping some ice cream or ringing up someone for five thousand dollars' worth of ice cream by accident.

Still, things were a little different now that Allie went to another school. When we used to see each other every day, we didn't seem to have any problems, but now that we saw her only one or two times a week, things were different. She was still my best friend, but I didn't know every detail of what was going on with her anymore.

I started snapping photos. First I took a picture of the menu sign where the flavors were written in colored chalk. I typed in the caption, Sprinkle Sundays squad goals: try a new flavor at Molly's #IceCream #Bayville #Yum, making sure to throw in some hashtags so people knew how to find the store.

Then I started snapping photos of the shop. It was *so* gorgeous that sometimes I wished I could live there. I took a photo of the vintage metal letters behind the freezers, with light bulbs in them that spelled out ICE CREAM. Then I got a wide shot of the parlor, with the cool black-and-white checkered floor flecked with gold; the high counter with stools looking out the window; and the three round, white tables surrounded by wire chairs. The chair cushions had blue- and cream-colored stripes, which matched the awning on the outside of the building.

There was so much to photograph! Above the register, light fixtures that looked like ice cream cones hung down from the ceiling. So cute! Then I moved on to the buckets inside the counter that held all of the toppings that customers could choose to put on their ice cream or have mixed in. I got a close-up of a bin of rainbow sprinkles, and then a jar of red and yellow and green gummy bears, and another one of some glistening blue gummy fish.

Then I grabbed Allie and Sierra and pulled us all together.

"Sprinkles selfie!" I cried, and I held out the phone and clicked.

"Let me see that before you post it!" Sierra said, grabbing the phone from me.

"Don't worry. You look gorgeous," I said, and I wasn't wrong. Sierra had an amazing smile.

I handed the phone to Sierra so that she could see.

"It's not *bad*," Sierra said, looking at it. "Just don't tag me." Then she continued scrolling through the photo feed on my phone. "Oh my gosh, I can't believe that outfit Jenna wore on Wednesday."

"I know! She looked stunning," I agreed.

"Jenna Robinson?" Allie said. "I thought she always wears jeans and sneakers."

"No, Jenna Horowitz," I corrected her. "Remember her? She was in my fifth-grade class."

Allie shrugged. "So, what was she wearing?"

"A black miniskirt and a long-sleeved white shirt

with a collar, and black ankle boots," Sierra reported. "It was so sophisticated!"

"Well, she did copy the whole outfit from the fall cover of *Teen Trend* magazine, so minus ten points for being unoriginal," I pointed out. "But only Jenna would have the guts to wear it, so ten points added."

I liked to pretend to score people's outfits, almost like I really *was* a TV show host.

"Speaking of guts, did you read that chapter about the digestive system in biology?" Sierra asked. "That was so gross. But Mr. Bongort made it really funny, thank goodness."

"Yeah, he was joking around the whole time," I replied. "Cole was picked to reenact the bathroom bit in class," I added for Allie's benefit. "It was hysterical."

"Cole is so annoying," Sierra said. "But it was pretty funny, watching him not be able to find a bathroom fast enough!"

"Well, I wouldn't know," Allie chimed in, and there was that edge to her voice again.

Sierra and I exchanged looks. It was really hard for Allie when she felt left out.